KNOW WHEN TO RUN

MISSION 1

BLACK OCEAN: MIRTH & MAYHEM

J.S. MORIN

MAGICAL SCRIVENER PRESS

Magical Scrivener Press
www.magicalscrivener.com

Ordering Information: Special discounts are available on quantity purchases by corporations, associations, and others. For details, contact the publisher at the address above.

J.S. Morin — First Edition

ISBN: 978-1-64355-123-4

Printed in the United States of America

KNOW WHEN TO RUN

MISSION 1

A SHUTTLE LANDED with a coughing flare of ion engines and a cloud of dust. The vessel's hull bore a gilded crest out of keeping with its grim, battered exterior: an ornate letter C struck through with a bolt of stylized lightning. No sooner had the ship touched down in the midst of a grassy meadow than its boarding ramp descended.

The creak of protesting hydraulics cut short with the ramp less than halfway down.

"Confound it!" a crotchety voice echoed from inside, followed by a muttering of syllables not kept in common parlance since the age of pharaohs. Giving an even more tortured metallic wail, the ramp overpowered its pistons and slammed to the soil.

Grumbling beneath his breath as he marched down, Mordecai paused to shout back into the vessel's interior. "Percival, you'd better have this horseless skyship operating properly by the time I get back! I don't intend to spend one minute longer than necessity dictates on this untended golf course of a colony."

He didn't care whether the ramp sealed up or leaked air

when he got back. Mordecai was a wizard, and that came with certain allowances making do with what technologists couldn't live without. Lost air could be conjured. Heat could as easily come from the ship's fireplace as the mysterious vents that belched warm, breathable air from somewhere in the vessel's belly. All that mattered was that the engines pushed and the dratted computer could aim them home.

Mordecai The Brown had all his hair despite the first locks of gray creeping in among the black. The wrinkles at the corners of his eyes were more a product of a perpetual scowl than a consequence of age. He'd dressed for the wilderness, with shin-high boots and denim slacks. His blazer was cut from the current Earth fashions with the exception of sleeves wide enough to tuck opposite hands inside—which he did out of habit. Around his neck hung a medallion bearing an identical sigil to the one on the side of the ship.

The mark of the Convocation of Wizards.

"Now what's going on in there that you lot wouldn't say on scientific channels?" Mort demanded.

His hosts, two squirrelly men in flowing black robes with wide sleeves, didn't look up to meet his glare. "Grendel has locked every door to the manor. We lost six good men trying to get him out."

Mordecai took a step closer, and both his hosts tensed. "First things first, his name's not Grendel. It's Ricky. Ricky 'Trumpet Nose' Bronson. I went to school with him. I don't care if *you* lot buy his scary-monster sobriquet, but I've played dodgeball with him, and he was no good at it. Second, you didn't lose six good men. You lost six reckless idiots. Never go into a fight you can lose. Now... for that third matter..."

"Yes?" one of the other wizards asked meekly.

"You never answered my question. What's so special about

this one that the colonial yahoos didn't just bomb it from orbit? Isn't that their solution to everything?"

"Civilians."

Mordecai rolled his eyes. It wasn't a word commonly used by wizards to describe noncombatants. But it summed up both the military and political stance on those unable to defend themselves. It also explained why they'd summoned Convocation assistance from halfway across the galaxy rather than use a blunt instrument to solve their problems for them.

"So, in the nuttiest of nutshells, they're willing to let *me* inflict collateral damage so they can sit back, shrug, and let the Convocation take the blame."

Two heads nodded. Mordecai could imagine hearing the loose little brains rattling around inside them.

With a sigh, Mordecai turned his sights to the manor house. It lay a good half mile away, across uneven terrain riddled with slabs of rock and splashes of bog. The structure itself bore stylings of an English country house, right down to the hedgerows around the empty starship pad.

Turning toward his own vessel, Mordecai bellowed, "Percival! Why couldn't you have landed the bloody thing over *there*?" He pointed to the spot that lay within a cobbled walkway of their target.

"With all due respect, Guardian," one of the local wizards cut in. "We waved your pilot down here so we'd be safe to plan from a distance."

The other, silent until now, cleared his throat. "What, um, is the plan? Do you... need us to walk you through the—"

Mordecai was already trudging across the moor. "Nope. Just keep out of trouble."

His hosts scurried after him, subtly not fast enough to gain ground. "But we lost six—"

"Idiots. Yeah. You mentioned that. Look, Boston Prime didn't send you some fresh library aid, straight out of Oxford to bring back whatever little Ricky's been reading—or possibly writing—over yonder...

"They sent the Guardian of the Plundered Tomes."

A dry wind whipped across an open-air landing field. Chuck Ramsey squinted one eye and tried to keep the hull of the *Radio City* between him and the sand carried along with each gust. Lubeck IV wasn't exactly the kind of colony tourism boards promoted. Lubeck Delta wasn't even the nicest of the colony's cities.

"Hey, how much longer on those fuel rods?" he asked, shouting over the howl.

The mechanic wore weather-ruggedized datagoggles and coveralls. His voice came muffled by a filtration mask. "Had a helluva time getting the old ones out. Don't know what you did to 'em, but the color was way off."

Chuck grinned despite the light sandblasting his teeth got. "Guy on Carlsbad juiced the rods for me. Can't share the process. Promised 10 percent longer range, but I got 12. But what about the new ones? I got places to be. Gig on Orion."

"I caught your show last night." Chuck perked up. "I'm doing Orion a favor. No credit. Cash or digital, but you've either got the terras or you don't have fuel rods."

Despite the dig, Chuck didn't flinch at the criticism. After all, he knew he was an acquired taste.

"Look. If I don't make it to Orion by a week from tomorrow, there won't be terras to pay anyone anything. Who wins in that scenario?"

"Comedy bar patrons across the galaxy," the mechanic replied without missing a beat.

Chuck snickered. It was a good shot. If this guy had decided to heckle him last night, it might have improved what had admittedly been a lackluster show. "Look, friend. I know you're not in charge here. How about I make you a deal?"

Even through the dust storm and the datagoggles, Chuck couldn't mistake the mechanic's scowl. "What kind of deal?"

Circling around, Chuck put a conspiratorial hand on the man's shoulder. "I'll bet you a refund of your ticket that I can get your boss to spot me credit for a full set of fuel rods. Deal?"

Perhaps sensing that Chuck hadn't asked for anything if he won the bet, the mechanic jumped on the opportunity. "Deal."

Leaving the man with a few pats on the shoulder for reassurance, he pointed up to the traffic control tower. "I'll have boss-man give you a high-sign if he agrees. You wait here a minute."

"'Kay..." the mechanic replied, then stood there with his arms crossed as Chuck braved the dust storm on his way to the tower.

"Who colonizes these hellholes?" Chuck asked the storm when he was sure no human ears could hear him. There had to have been ten thousand better planets out there, planets with near Earth-identical gravity, planets with balmy climates and sandy beaches, planets developed with enough environmental domes to cover all the inhabitants.

Leaning into the wind, Chuck made his way to the control tower and punched the door control. He ducked inside gasping for breath. The tower's recirculating air supply blew fresh, clean, cool air that countered the inhospitable weather that had permeated Chuck's outer layer of skin.

A moment's glance searching for a lift only turned up a set of squared-spiral stairs leading up.

"Of course..." he grumbled. A colony that could afford lifts in public buildings would probably also pave their starports—and maybe construct windbreaks to keep ships on the leeward side of the storms.

On the way up, Chuck peeked in at the intervening floors. There was some kind of break room or cafeteria, an office, equipment storage. He could work with this.

At the top floor, Chuck encountered the traffic controller and owner of the shipyard. A quick glance at the name plate on the guy's workstation identified him as Garson Smalls.

"Hi, Garson? Chuck Ramsey. Got a minute?" It took all his willpower not to make light of the man's name and work in a French waiter joke.

"Who?"

"Comedian Chuck Ramsey, captain of the *Radio City*, currently ready for departure on pad 22."

Garson was a leathery specimen of colonist, looking like he'd spent a few too many unprotected days out in the dust. A local, no doubt, not an itinerant spacer job-hopping the galaxy. He nodded when the pad number clicked. "Oh yeah. The one looking to buy fuel rods on credit. What is this? A One Church charity operation? Scram. Come back when you can pay."

Chuck waved away the notion with both hands, crestfallen that the traffic controller could insinuate he might be looking for a handout. "No. Nothing like that. But your ground team already pulled my old fuel rods. I think there might be enough oomph in them to get me to Mallostar. I was gonna offer your guy 20T to plug them back in so I could get out of here. But he wanted the OK from you first. Can you just give him a wave? I already handed him a hardcoin twenty in good faith."

In only took Garson a second before he sighed and stood from his chair. He leaned close to the window and waved until the mechanic waved back. "There. Good luck limping to Mallostar."

The cockpit of the *Radio City* echoed with the sounds of guitar strings. Becky Ramsey sat with an antique acoustic perched in her lap, strumming chords to an Early Data Era classic. It was less the kind of antique that appreciated in value and more the kind that had been forgotten in a rented storage locker and purchased on the cheap at auction. Years of mistreatment at a prior owner's hands had left the body scratched and the neck slightly warped, but it kept tuned for a few hours at a time. Becky would have sung along, but getting lost in a song usually got her closing her eyes, and she was on watch.

From the pilot's chair, the *Radio City* offered a wide forward view of its surroundings. Floor-to-ceiling, the windshield presented a flat front that played havoc on the craft in atmosphere but was great for sightseeing at low speeds. Out in the Black Ocean, some careful maneuvering could result in spectacular viewing angles.

For now, the front window aimed squarely toward the control tower of the Lubeck Delta landing yard.

She'd seen the wave from the regional traffic controller. The thumps and clanks from the hull made it clear that someone out there was working on installing fresh fuel rods. From here on out, it was a waiting game.

"Mom?" Brad called out from behind her. Becky turned to find her oldest son approaching.

Whip thin and gawky, Brad looked like he'd never met a comb or a clothes processor. His oversized boots clomped on the deck plates, but they'd hopefully last him the year before he outgrew them. Not that Brad seemed like he was in any danger of becoming a giant. But over the past year or so, he'd gone from a scrawny runt to just regular scrawny.

"How much longer until Dad gets back?"

Something in the innocence of that question made Becky instantly suspicious. "Where's your sister? I asked you to watch her."

"Mike's on it."

The notion of leaving a five-year-old to watch his three-year-old sister didn't inspire confidence. "Your dad'll be back any minute. Now scoot. I've got to be ready up here."

"Make you a deal..."

Becky's blood ran cold. "What kind of deal?"

"I'll watch for Dad if you make Rhi's cookie-snacks."

Becky checked the landing field. No sign of Chuck yet. "Is that what this is about? You don't want to work the food processor?"

"And you don't want to sit here playing *Blowin' in the Wind* off tempo while you watch a door."

"I wasn't off—" Becky caught herself before letting her son sidetrack her. He was getting to be as bad as Chuck. "Fine. But when you spot him, yell. And... start the engines."

Brad spread his hands. "Hey, no problem."

They scooted past one another, and Brad wriggled into the pilot's chair.

▭

Brad Ramsey cracked his knuckles and took hold of the flight yoke in both hands. The grips were too large, suited for Dad's hands better than either his or Mom's, but he'd gotten used to them. Not that it mattered, since the *Radio City* was parked with the engines off. Even Mom couldn't object as he twisted and pulled, mimicking the motions of a deep-space dogfight that the unarmed *Radio City* couldn't begin to participate in.

Noting that Mom had left her guitar on the co-pilot's seat, Brad hefted it and strummed a few open chords.

"Definitely out of tune," he pronounced. Plucking the strings one at a time, he set about tweaking each to get them playing proper notes. The longer he kept at it, the worse it all sounded. Finally, after a test strum that resulted in a particularly grating chord, he set the instrument back down and positioned it as if he'd never touched it.

When he looked up, Dad was out in the wind, running toward the *Radio City*. One arm raised, he circled a finger in the air in the whirly-bird "spin up the engines" sign.

"Well, shit." Brad had missed his father's exit from the control tower. Clearly, Dad was in a huge hurry, too, since Dad *never* ran unless someone was after him. "I can't possibly get Mom over here in time."

The words were an argument to himself, and he made a good point. There really wasn't a choice.

Flicking through the pre-flight without hesitation, the *Radio City* flared to life. Engines hummed. The floor buzzed. Outside the ship, men's voices shouted in anger, their exact words lost in the commotion.

Remembering that they were here for fuel, Brad checked the fuel gauge. Three of the four slots showed full. The fourth was blank, indicating no fuel rod present at all. Also, there was a blinking warning that the fuel panel hadn't been closed.

Shrugging in resignation, Brad eased open the throttle and lifted the *Radio City* off the ground. Gingerly, he gave it a little forward thrust and lurched toward the running parent heading the other way.

Taking his eyes off the landing field, he reached over and flipped first the vacuum interlock then the control to fold down the passenger ramp. It wasn't a long trip to rendezvous with his dad, so Brad immediately started a 270 degree right turn to bring the ramp around without slinging the unsecured fuel rods out of the *Radio City*.

"BRAD! BRAAAAAAAD! Bradley Carlin Ramsey, what do you think you're doing?" Becky shrieked as she raced back to the cockpit.

"Hold your horses," Brad replied casually. He watched the altimeter as it self-corrected its data range to include fractions of meters. With the deft touch of a surgeon, he brought the vessel to a quarter of a meter off the ground and held steady.

"I'm in!" Dad bellowed. "Hit it, kid!"

Not needing to be told twice, Brad slammed the throttle to full, not pulling back on the yoke until they passed the control tower, letting the ion wash kick up a storm that would blind visual contact briefly.

"How did you know Brad was flying?" Mom demanded.

"No need to apologize," Dad assured her jovially. "I'm fine. Kid stepped in and covered for you."

"But how did you know it wasn't me?"

Even with his eyes on the approaching stars, Brad knew Dad's shrug well enough to picture it. "Kid's got panache. Don't get me wrong, you fly great. But... without the panache. Phew. I could use a beer."

"You don't wanna take over?" Brad asked, a thrill building in his belly.

"Nah. You're doing swell."

Brad's eyes lit. This was it. He was flying for real. Sure, he'd flown all over colonial space, landed dozens of times, docked with space stations, and gotten to play around with deep-space maneuvering.

But this was the first time he'd piloted a getaway.

"*Vessel* Radiocity, *this is Lubeck Planetary Security. We've got a report that you just burned out of Lubeck Delta with an unpaid fuel tab.*"

Brad turned to look back into the ship.

Beer in hand, Dad perked up. "You need me to tag in, buddy?"

Without stopping to think himself out of it, Brad replied, "I've got it."

An aftermarket addition clung to the dashboard like a parasite just above the comm system. Foreign cables disappeared into the console through inexpertly drilled holes. Brad activated the voice scrambler and spun the indicator dial to a random setting.

"We've got a medical thing here. Big time emergency," he replied to the planetary security officer. Thanks to the scrambler, he sounded like a woman with a sore throat.

"*If you need medical assistance, we can—*"

"Thanks. No. Did I say medical? I mean magical. We've got some kind of sticky gremlin on board that we can't allow loose." If that didn't sum up his sister Rhiannon, he didn't know what did. "Hang back, just in case we need to self-destruct."

"*Self-destruct? What are you talking about?*"

Brad kept an eye on the *Radio City's* distance from the planet's surface. It wouldn't be long before they were far enough to drop into astral space. At two hundred kilometers, it was safe to transition out of realspace. They had more than a hundred left to go, but with the atmosphere barely a factor anymore, they were closing that gap fast.

His breath was coming quick when Brad opened the comm again to stall. "*Hold on. Can I get back to you in like* five *minutes? This thing is crapping on the floor, and I think it's hungry again.*"

Watching the range count down, Brad fired the reverse thrusters. They had to be at a dead stop or at least super close. Nobody actually knew how the magical devices worked—nobody but wizards, anyway. But everyone knew you couldn't transition on the move.

On the sensors, Brad watched a sentry ship close in on him. But the vector wasn't a direct intercept. The security forces were pulling alongside to see what happened with the bizarre, magically infested ship leaving their gravity well.

"So long, losers," Brad said, belatedly checking to verify that he had, in fact, not been speaking on an open channel.

Setting the star-drive to a not-quite-legal 3.5 Astral Units, he dropped the *Radio City* out of realspace.

Stars faded from view. The planet vanished. A flat, listless gray enveloped the vessel.

"Not bad," Dad commented from just behind him, startling Brad, who hadn't heard the approach. "I'd have stuck with the medical thing, but you kept them off balance long enough. But tell me, what would you have done if they'd followed?"

"That was a Starbear '29. No way that heap was dropping below 2 AU."

Dad nodded solemnly along with that logic. "And if they had? If they'd boarded us?"

"I'd have let you take over."

With a chuckle, Dad tousled Brad's hair. "And don't you forget it."

Brad rose from the pilot's chair. "You taking the helm?"

Beer in one hand, Dad rubbed his chin with the other. "Nah. Flying's a hassle. You can handle the easy part."

The nav computer already had the destination of Dad's next gig plugged in. Not that coordinates consisting of all zeroes would be hard for *anyone* to forget. Brad turned the autopilot on and launched them on their journey.

"Earth, here we come!"

Mordecai had his feet up on the cushion of an ottoman, a tankard of warm beer half-empty in his hand. A low fire cast a warm glow throughout the room, throwing cozy shadows behind the furnishings and keeping the scientific coldness at bay. With a trifling of his copious imagination, he could ignore being cooped up inside a flying metal space box.

A leather-bound volume rested on the ottoman beside his booted feet. Thick chains bound it shut, not that it was a particularly dangerous specimen. Convocation protocols deemed it a prudent measure to enact in the transportation of any plundered tome. Dark wizards popped up all the time. Most kept some record of their life's work, ranging from scattered sheafs of paper that the Convocation would bind into proper volumes to sprawling manifestos that resembled sets of encyclopediae.

His favorite find in his young career had been the collected works of Guiseppe of Neo Avalon. A man holding the dual pretentions of an ancient royal ancestry and literary prowess, his research had been written in the form of an annotated biography. Early drafts had scattered his lair, and the finished version had been both entertaining and chilling at the same time. Reading the man's descent from curiosity to mania over the application of various elixirs to unwitting subjects had proved the fineness of the line any wizard walked between power and madness.

Ricky's Big Book of Animals was a horror show, no doubt, but it wasn't a particularly thorough examination of the subject. Mordecai knew enough to infer how the loudmouthed twit had been forcing copulation between humans and animals to produce monsters in the finest tradition of Greek myth. Anyone with a proper education could have.

Ricky Bronson had lacked in virtuosity.

While Mordecai had never begrudged a wizard going rotten over a truly remarkable idea, he hated the pedestrian pikers who went bad for the sake of indulging a wanton streak. Stopping someone from digging up the brain of a Mesopotamian god and reanimating it in the flesh of a dinosaur... Mordecai had been half tempted to let old Horus Johnson have a crack at seeing if it worked before killing him.

Guys like Ricky, they were just a day at the office. A day away from the library—actually, a full week away—but it just amounted to a chore that pulled him away from Nancy and the kids.

Percival entered from the cockpit. "Sir, we're about to arrive."

"Need me to...?" He waggled his fingers.

"The star-drive can handle the return to realspace, sir."

Mordecai arched an eyebrow. "Can it?"

Percival sighed. "Yes, Guardian. You didn't put us so far down that I can't get us back. We're not stranded and at the mercy of Astral Search and Rescue."

With a snicker, Mordecai conceded. "That's why I like you, Percy. Louis and Geneva always try to make it sound like the planets would stop spinning if I wasn't around."

"I would never sink to base patronization, sir," Percival deadpanned. He sketched a half-hearted bow and returned to the cockpit, calling over his shoulder, "We'll be on terra firma in roughly twenty-three minutes."

Ah, Earth.

Home.

Also home to thirty billion technologists all trying to believe magic out of existence with their zombified techno-worship. Not that most of them even realized. The summation of scientific brainpower across the globe lumbered on its narrow-minded course, trampling creativity in its path. They came up with a thousand different names for elemental earth, tried to cage gravity with numbers, traded machines with one another to overcome their basic ignorance of conjuration, levitation, and fire-starting.

When the wall of the ship's living room folded into a set of stairs, Mordecai swung his feet to the floor, drained the last of his beer, and collected his trophy.

The campus of Harvard University enveloped him, a sanctuary of magic in a world dominated by scientists. Its brick buildings and manicured grasses hearkened back to a time when space travel was a children's story and wizards and scientists pretended one another didn't exist.

Louis was waiting for him on the landing pad. The tech liaison wore wizard robes but with close-fitting sleeves that showed his hands were no threat to the scientific devices around him. Had he worn a garment in which to hide them, he might not have looked quite as nervous as he wrung his hands.

"It's a book, Louis. If you're afraid of it, don't open it,"

Mordecai said, thrusting the volume toward the lackey with a jangle of iron chains. Louis recoiled, but Mordecai didn't foist the book onto him. "Relax. It's not even going in the vault. It's just the pedestrian ramblings of a second-rate psychopath."

"It's... it's not that, Guardian," Louis said.

"Then what? Spit it out, man. I've been packed in a tuna fish can for a week now with only an hour's respite to incinerate some chimaeric monsters and their creator. Frankly, I'd been looking forward to seeing my wife here when I got back, not you. No offense..." He paused a second. "Not much, anyway."

"It's Nebuchadnezzar."

Mordecai slumped his shoulders and let out a sigh. "What did that old coot do now? Do you need someone to chase him out of the undergraduate dorms again?" Then, mind still tossing around possibilities, he scowled. "Does he have clothes on?"

"He's dying."

Mordecai huffed and strode past Louis. "Depending who you talk to, Nebuchadnezzar The Brown has been dying for the better part of two decades. Just watch. In a week, he'll have concocted some new charm and be running around embarrassing the family all over again."

Louis scurried to keep pace as Mordecai marched toward the library. "Not this time. Your whole family's gotten together."

That rooted Mordecai's feet to the bricks. He cast Louis an arched glare. "Even Gilly?"

"Your cousin Gilgamesh arrived this morning."

Mordecai rubbed his chin. If Gilly had returned from his terraforming assignment, this had to be serious. Terramancers were notorious sticklers for schedules. If it were an uncle or even a sibling, Gilly might have been instructed to wait for a favorable juncture in the project to attend a belated memorial service. With Nebuchadnezzar being a former First Chair of the Convocation, he warranted special deathbed dispensation.

When Mordecai turned on his heel and headed toward his grandparents' home, just off campus, Louis caught up with him. "Do you... do you need me to... to..." He kept his arm tucked against his chest as he pointed at the chained book in Mordecai's grasp.

With a harrumph, Mordecai shifted the book and tucked it beneath the other arm. "I'll bring it with me. You can get back to work."

"Thank you, sir." Without a breath's hesitation, Louis made himself scarce. Not that Mordecai expected any further work from the man the rest of the day. If he managed to make his way back to the library today, he fully expected to find Louis tankard-deep in herbal tea so strong it bordered on hallucinogenic.

With a pleasant fall morning and a brisk pace, Mordecai spent an enjoyable five minutes trekking on foot to the stately Boston Prime home of Nebuchadnezzar and Isadora Brown.

Servants milled outside and ushered Mordecai in as soon as he arrived.

"He's been asking for you," Harald, Grandfather's butler, informed him. "He's been quite insistent."

Nancy intercepted him as Mordecai made his way through a premature wake being held in the halls of his grandparents' home. She hugged him, heedless of the chained literary atrocity he carried. "I'm so glad you made it in time."

"What's different this time? He was healthy as a dragon when I left."

Nancy let out an eloquent sigh. "Let him tell the story. I...

I don't know if I'd get the details sorted." She pulled back and glanced down at the book. "Need me to hang onto that?"

With an amused snort, Mordecai handed it over. "Wouldn't want to distract the old coot with shop talk."

Cousins, aunts, nieces, and nephews parted to make way. Only his great-uncle Solomon declined to yield, standing guard at his brother's bedroom door. "Don't go upsetting him. You know how he gets."

Stepping right up to look his uncle Sol in the eye, Mordecai dared the old man to meet his gaze. But Uncle Sol looked aside. Then, cowed, he stepped out of the way. Ten years ago, that confrontation would have gone differently. It was a generally accepted truism that wizards grew in power with age.

Some wizards just grew quicker than others.

Mordecai opened the inlaid wooden door and entered his grandfather's bedchamber.

The stone-walled room did its level best to keep eight centuries of architectural progress at bay. Shadows skulked in every corner as smokeless fires in the hearth and torches in wall sconces flickered. The furnishings were Louis XIV—no relation to Louis Cramer, inept library lackey, as best Mort knew. While the other side of the house looked out onto modern Boston Prime streets rife with tech and the trappings of science, the view through the balcony door was the quaint, pastoral campus of the neighboring university. An ornate four-poster bed anchored the room, velvet drapes parted to reveal an elderly wizard in his bathrobe, tucked to the waist beneath embroidered blankets.

"About time," Nebuchadnezzar scolded, then coughed.

While Mordecai had been expecting to find his grandfather full of piss and vinegar, the old bugger was clearly worse off than his imagination had predicted. Sallow skin wasn't a mere trick of the light, and there was a hollowness to the man's cheeks.

Nebuchadnezzar snapped his fingers. There was no sound as frail bones and dry skin robbed the gesture of its vigor. Nevertheless, Mort felt a change. The old wizard's will encircled them both with the sensation of an inaudible "pop."

They were alone before, but now they were shielded against eavesdropping of all kinds.

"What'd you do this time?" Mordecai asked acidly. There was no family theater performance to put on. The two had bonded over a common animosity toward Mordecai's father. No pretense was needed. No punches would be pulled. "Necromancy? Demonology? Looks like you lost ground."

Nebuchadnezzar tried to chuckle and instead broke down into a wheezing fit. "Limited form of chronomancy—though don't breathe a word of that outside these walls."

"Naturally." There were few forms of magic the Convocation abhorred more than tinkering with time. As a former Guardian himself, Nebuchadnezzar knew how many half-baked theories on time magic were in the vault. None of them worked. Given that the Grim Reaper seemed intent on collecting this particular dark wizard himself, Mordecai didn't feel any need to exert his authority as present-day Guardian of the Plundered Tomes. "So, what went wrong?"

"What didn't?" Nebuchadnezzar snapped. "Pendular's Theorem was fabricated. Slogged through all that drivel about losing his daughter, and the good bits were either pure fiction or untested hypotheses. Almost makes me think he *wanted* to die and wrote the thing just so I'd save him the scandal of a suicide. Then... hoo boy... it turns out that transferring life energy to an Aetheron crystal for safekeeping isn't reversible if you overload the crystal."

"Where did you get a—never mind. You made your own, didn't you?"

Nebuchadnezzar raised his thin shoulders in a shrug. "Seemed less risky than asking someone to steal into the Vault of Alexandria for one."

Mordecai folded his arms and fixed his grandfather with a stern glare. "Thus, your story ends. I trust you asked me here to clean up any evidence, so no one spoils your funeral with an investigation into dark wizardry." If it came to that point, Mordecai would be forced by the Council to recuse himself. They'd need to get out in front of this.

Instead, Nebuchadnezzar shook his head. "No. I asked you here for a bigger favor than that."

"Bigger than betraying my vows and aiding dark wizardry?"

Nebuchadnezzar scoffed. "Teensy potatoes. Guardians have been covering up for well-connected dark wizards for millennia. No. I have one last chance to cheat death. It requires help only you can provide."

Mordecai arched one eyebrow. "Oh. What kind of help?"

"I need you—in a very, *very* specific way—to kill me."

The great gray nothingness of astral space swarmed with shipping traffic. Ghostly, insubstantial, other vessels flitted past the stationary *Radio City*. Chuck Ramsey shooed his eldest son from the pilot's chair with a grumble.

"What'd you do to it? It was working when we left."

"Nothing. I just hit the button," Brad replied, pointing to the correct spot on the console to return them to realspace.

"You must have pushed it wrong," Chuck insisted, gesturing to the astral depth indicator that read 2.91 AU. "Otherwise, we'd be able to see Earth in all its hypercrowded glory."

"And money," Brad added dutifully.

Chuck wagged a finger. Kid was right on that count. "The skies of Earth are paved in terras," he quoted the old saying. Then he scowled. "But not if we can't get there."

Leaning across the comm console, Brad pressed close to the window. "Looks smooth as buttered ice out there." A swarm of other vessels, mostly transports and cargo ships, raced past like a colossal holovid field.

For a moment, Chuck watched along with his son. Without being at *quite* the same astral depth, it was a wizard's guess as to whether those ships saw them in return or whether they could collide. He hovered his finger over the astral controls. "Don't get used to it. Once I get us back to realspace..." He paused for dramatic effect as he jabbed the button to bring them out of astral. Nothing happened. "I *said*... once I get us back to realspace..."

Several more attempts and the button performed no better.

"Boo," Brad taunted, cupping his hands around his mouth to mimic a hostile crowd. "Send in the jugglers."

Chuck aimed a mock warning finger at him. "Don't ever do that when I'm on stage. Last thing I need is to finally make Comedy Daily—as the opening act for a team of laaku plasma-wrench jugglers."

"Those guys were good."

No shit, they were good. With bodies akin to chimpanzees and equally dexterous with every limb, the laaku people were naturals when it came to the performing physical arts. Chuck was careful not to get himself booked at any venue where he might be compared to a truly mesmerizing act. Going back-to-back with Noru of Abasi and his quadrijuggling pals had been disastrous.

Just then, the comm barked at them. "*Vessel* Radiocity, *this is Earth Astral Control. We're scanning you at a non-standard 2.91 depth. Please adjust your star-drive to an approved travel lane.*"

Huffing a sigh of frustration, Chuck responded on the same channel. "Look, I know what it says on our registration, but that's an error. It's the *Radio City*. Two words. Maybe you could put in a good word with the Registry of Spacefaring Vehicles and get them to fix it."

"*Sir, we don't work for the RSV.*"

"Not even if I added an RSV-please?"

"*Sir, please get yourself to a standard astral depth. I can't have you impeding solar traffic.*"

Chuck ran his fingers through his hair. This guy just wouldn't be sidetracked. "Look. We're on it. Our star-drive's just a little finicky. Give us a few minutes to—"

"*I'm dispatching Search and Rescue to render assistance. They'll tow you to realspace for repairs.*"

Somewhere in the digital void, Chuck's bank account screamed. Sol was a black hole for terras; Earth doubly so. He couldn't start this tour out in the red. "No-no-no. Don't go to the trouble. Like I said—"

"*Await instruction from Search and Rescue. Earth Astral Control out.*"

The comm cut off.

"Don't look at me," Brad said, holding up his hands. "I spend anything I get."

That much was true. Brad had flatly refused to save for a rainy day, claiming—accurately—that they weren't planetside enough to worry about rain. Between that and the couple times Chuck had been forced to reacquire allowance money to pay for fuel rods, there was little chance Brad would ever be available for a quick loan again.

Slumping into the pilot's chair, Chuck sullenly pressed the same button on the astral console again and again every few seconds.

Brad made himself scarce.

After a few minutes, the comm squawked again. "*Vessel* Radiocity, *I'm Lieutenant Jessinda Chan with Search and Rescue. Power down and we'll have you in realspace in no time.*"

With a simple re-targeting of his mindless tapping, Chuck hit the comm and held it. Forcing his best stage voice, he replied with hollow chipperness, "Thanks, Lieutenant. Much obliged."

Then he took a swipe at the dashboard that killed the engines and maneuvering thrusters—plus the life support system. Chuck hurriedly turned the latter back on before slouching back and waiting for a tow that would probably cost him more than he was due to make this whole trip.

The peasant folk of Boston Prime called it Merlin's Private Library. The great fount of wisdom collected by the Convocation wasn't open to casual visitors, though members found it a trivial matter to gain admittance. Neither had the famed master magician of Camelot ever set foot in the place, as best anyone could tell. Though the tapestries on the wall dated to medieval times, the building was newer than his era.

Each time Mordecai crossed the threshold of the great library, he felt the weighty pressure of the scientific world around him ease. The stonework had an ancient presence, a gravitas all its own that denied the headlong rush of science as it gobbled up the souls of the mindless to fuel its own ambitions. Today, however, that calm was tinged with the burden Nebuchadnezzar had foisted onto him.

"Guardian," a prim, chipper voice called out as he made his way through the grand foyer. It belonged to the chief modern archivist. "You'll never guess what I acquired just this morning."

"I dunno, Elliot. What?" Mordedcai grumbled without slowing his pace. The archivist fell into step a pace behind.

Elliot wore a wide-sleeved tweed jacket and matching slacks. With his unkempt hair and wire-rimmed spectacles, he looked every bit the useless academic. "A complete set of Megami's Transposition Theorems. All five volumes!"

Without even looking at the man, Mordecai inquired, "The fakes someone's been peddling out of Mars, or the real McCoy?"

The footsteps trailing him slowed, then stopped.

"Fakes?"

Mordecai shook his head in disgust.

"I'm sorry to hear about Nebuchadnezzar," Elliot called after him. "How is the old boy?"

"He's as close to death today as he will be tomorrow," Mordecai barked back.

A part of him, deep down, reveled in lying with the truth. While he rarely partook in holovids—drivel for the slack-jawed masses—he could see the appeal when criminals tested their prowess against a clever investigator. Leave just enough clues to induce madness, not enough to get caught. Of course, the flash-and-grin crowd out in Hollyworld only told the stories where the law won.

Wizards knew better.

Both now and tomorrow, Mordecai suspected that his grandfather would be—roughly speaking—half a day away from dying. Tomorrow, he'd merely be on the far side.

Down a set of spiraling stone stairs, Mordecai descended into the copious basement of the library. His footsteps scuffed and echoed. Elliot didn't try to follow him down. Most of the librarians avoided the secure section of the building as a matter of decorum more than genuine fear, though several acted as though feral dogs were kept down there instead of books.

Though the wooden door at the bottom of the stairs was bound in iron set with a keyhole, there was no corresponding key. Mordecai traced a rune around where some oaf might think to stick a key. The door, used to the routine, opened just before he finished.

"Could've saved me the trouble," he muttered to it as he passed.

In the oppressive silence, lonely signs of habitation stood out. Down among the rows of shelves with books chained in captivity, a lone voice sang a children's educational song—something about numbers of different fruits and what animals would eat them.

Not making any effort to quiet his entry, it wasn't long before Mordecai's approach drew notice. The singer halted and called out, "Who's there?"

"Just me, Bast. What was that you were singing?"

Bast ducked her head out from one of the rows and cast Mordecai a puzzled look. "Was I? Oh, that. Nathaniel keeps letting the kids watch holovids. Guess the tunes are a little too catchy for their own good."

Mordecai smiled as best he could manage, given the pall upon his mood. "Go on. Take the rest of the night off."

"But I just got here. And Azrael's in Shanghai until—"

Diligence among the staff was all well and good, but tonight Mordecai neither needed nor wanted an audience. He stilled her protests with a raised hand. "Don't worry. I'll man the stacks tonight."

"You? Personally?"

Mordecai arched an eyebrow. "I'd do it impersonally, but I'm feeling like I'm inside my own head tonight."

There came a point in a wizard's career—usually much later in life than Mordecai currently found himself—when a wizard's casual, sneering wit often found itself misinterpreted as profound insight.

Bast emerged into the center aisle, head down and clutching a copy of the *Daemonicon Lecce* to her chest. "I'm sorry, sir. I didn't mean to infer that you weren't fully capable of... of—I'm sorry your grandfather isn't well."

Librarians were infrequently chosen for their tact and glib tongues. Mordecai simply gestured for her to hand over the book. "Go home. Sing to your kids."

"Do I have to?" Bast asked meekly.

"No," Mordecai replied. "But I want some solitude tonight. So scoot. Hire a sitter and take Nathaniel bowling or something."

"Thank you, sir." Bast made herself scarce. Mordecai didn't budge until the door closed behind her and the scuffing of her shoes on the stairs faded from hearing.

It was a quick detour to replace the *Daemonicon Lecce* back in place on its shelf. A dry piece of esoterica, the tome had been penned in the author's own blood. Written by a possessed monk in the 15th century, it contained the daily musings of the occupying demon. While not, in the strictest sense, a magical volume, it was the sort of mundane horror that would have served as an ideal bedtime story for parents who never wanted their children to sleep again.

Nancy had forbidden him from bringing it home for just that reason.

Mordecai tried to hold that notion in his head as he made his way to the vault. The melancholy atrocities contemplated by a bored, bourgeois demon unable to escape his human host would indeed seem like a children's fairytale before this night was over.

Nestled in the shadows of an already-gloomy basement, a heavy steel door adorned in Norse runes dominated an even deeper penumbra.

"Just stopping in for a look-see."

The runes yielded to Mordecai's casual greeting. Sickly green glows traced the worn carvings as glyphs lit one by one.

An orb of pale blue light appeared above Mordecai's upraised palm, hanging in place at his side as he ventured within.

The Vault of Plundered Tomes was the meat and gravy of the library's collection. The books upstairs had been printed, copied, and recopied ad nauseam, even into scientific formats in some cases. Advanced and culturally hot-button volumes might not see wide distribution, but wizards with proper credentials could lay their hands on one when needed.

Down here were the bad apples.

Wizards got themselves killed for writing literature like this. Oh, a mundane subversive could cause a fuss—or even kindle a revolution—with mere words spread among the magicless rabble. But none of those dealt in commandeering the immortal soul, altering history, or activating dormant volcanoes. The Vault of the Plundered Tomes contained works on those subjects and many more. Sure, the majority didn't work as fully or flawlessly as intended, but they still gave rotten ideas that could spoil nice wizards and possibly be combined with other failed ideas to piece together a Frankenstein's spellbook of real trouble.

A few, however, worked all too well already.

Tucked away on a shelf just inside the door, locked behind a small iron cell door with several of its ilk, rested the book Mordecai had pawned off on Nancy earlier. She didn't like it down among the plundered tomes, let alone the vault, but it would have been a short walk for her to have passed it along to a librarian. Apparently, when Mordecai wasn't around to say otherwise, any incoming volume entered quarantine. Right now, the unduly sequestered tome wasn't his concern.

The new book wasn't what Mordecai had come to see.

His aim lay at the back of the vault, behind yet another cage door, this one the full height of a man. It, too, yielded readily to the wizard charged with keeping grasping hands and greedy eyes at bay. Beyond it lay the books that worked.

Many of the spells and rituals contained in these volumes were simply bad ideas. One turned royal blood to gold—and only worked when it was still in the veins. Another allowed any two creatures to procreate and counted among the Convocation's most embarrassing scandals. An entire shelf was lined with books on reanimating the dead—a subject so rudimentary in its wickedness that the Convocation had been stamping it out since its inception and would likely continue doing so until it dissolved.

One, it was believed, had been written by creatures older than Earth itself.

By wizards' standards, Mordecai wasn't superstitious. He'd always believed the book's origin to be a myth. Nebuchadnezzar had convinced him otherwise.

The old coot had studied it years ago, taking a daft number of precautions and working entirely through intermediaries such as mirrors, lenses, and shadows. The book, from its leather binding to its vellum of questionable provenance, was only centuries old. The contents, however, had been reproduced faithfully—as best Nebuchadnezzar could tell—from origins before time had been invented.

Mordecai dismissed one final ward and hefted the *Tome of Bleeding Thoughts*.

Sweat beaded at Mordecai's brow.

He could turn the old man down. The request had been ludicrous, in keeping with Nebuchadnezzar's reputation as a gambler and schemer. Mordecai didn't have to play along. No one but his grandfather would ever know he'd denied a deathbed request.

Mordecai stormed out of the vault, leaving the door ajar behind him, and slammed the tome down on one of the reading tables. "I am Mordecai The Brown, Guardian of the Plundered Tomes. And if Nebuchadnezzar thinks I'm wizard enough to read you, then damn it, I'm not going to prove him wrong."

Steeling himself for what he might see inside, Mordecai opened the cover.

Inside, the scrawled symbols were beyond gibberish. Runes crawled within runes. Glyphs overwrote adjacent glyphs. Lines swam in his vision. Were they moving, or was he hallucinating? The line between those two possibilities blurred.

With a vague, almost secondhand accounting of his actions, Mordecai turned the pages and the patterns within seared themselves into the flesh of his brain. He read nothing. The book read itself to him as a nightmarish bedtime story. His eyes didn't blink. His thoughts ground to a halt. An entire language unfolded within him, sweeping clear unused spaces in his mind and setting up house.

How much time passed since opening the cover, Mordecai couldn't say. When the back cover slammed shut, and his trance ended, he needed to take a piss and he was famished. Breathing heavily, the horrors of what he'd read began to sink into his conscious mind.

"Not for all the gold in Atlantis," he told himself as he lurched toward the vault to return it. His feet remained glued to the floor. Was the book thwarting him? Did it not want to go back into captivity? What would happen if this monstrosity got loose?

He couldn't take it with him.

It didn't want to go back.

The things he could do, thanks to this vile tome. The things he knew that he could never unlearn, could never forget even in the tiniest detail. Other books among the plundered tomes might cause minor troubles if loosed into the wild. This one would be a calamity. What minds it didn't destroy outright through careless, thoughtless mystical might would be corrupted, saddled with temptations that no wizard should be forced to live with.

Before weakness overtook him, Mordecai set the book ablaze, still clutched in his hands. The Order of Prometheus taught an incantation that conjured unquenchable fire, fire that gnawed and ate and burned through damn near anything. Mordecai could summon it with a thought and did just that.

The *Tome of Bleeding Thoughts* didn't want to be destroyed. But its cover was closed. Whatever taint it had left in Mordecai's mind, his actions were his own. He dropped the book just before the fires touched his own fingers.

With a wordless snarl, he intensified the miniature inferno until naught but an oily dust was left to rain down to the floor.

Rubbing his chin, Mordecai pondered how he was going to cover this up. "No time. There'll be hell to pay one way or the other."

With the library basement's overnight staff off duty, he left the vault open and raced to make it back to his grandparents' home before it was too late.

The stage lights, in imitation of the old theaters of the Early Data Era, shone in Chuck's eyes to the point where he could barely make out the audience beyond the front couple rows. That hardly mattered. It also helped him ignore the fact that, beyond those first few rows, empty seats abounded.

Yet, the show had to go on. "And so, I get back from selling my starship and the banker tells me, 'yeah, now you qualify for a star-drive repair loan.' Except the loan won't even cover buying the ship back and I'm out 5,000T in the end. Bankers... lemme tell ya."

A few laughs tittered back from the crowd.

"And don't get me started on financial planners. I responded to one of those free ads—you know the ones in all the tram stations? Make an appointment. Sit down. This kid fresh out of college starts telling me all this crazy stuff about investing and saving and I go, 'Whoa, hold on. I just want you to help set me up so I don't have to worry about money in my old age.'"

"*Too late,*" someone in the back of the theater shouted out.

Chuck shot the guy a wink and a pointed finger—guessing on the aim thanks to the glare—before pressing on. "So, to my surprise, the kid pulls out a blaster. Slides it across the desk. 'What's this for?' I ask him. 'Well, I looked at your financial records, and you've got two choices. Either shoot yourself now or go rob a bank.'"

Chuck waited for the scattered laughs to die down as he timed the punchline.

"So, here I still am, and I've got an early appointment in front of a judge tomorrow. Goodnight folks! You've been swell!"

He raised the hand that wasn't holding his portable microphone and waved to the crowd during a polite wash of applause.

As soon as he was safely backstage, he handed the mic to one of the theater staff and slumped. Becky met him with a beer, top already popped.

"Thanks, babe."

The backstage area buzzed with activity. Other performers bustled in a frenzy of preparation for their upcoming acts, many, like the Ramseys, had their whole families along, giving the area undertones of a daycare center. Navigating the fluid chaos of bodies, Chuck retrieved a towel and patted his forehead before chugging his beer.

"Set went well," Becky ventured.

"'Well'?" Chuck scoffed. "I hope the critics out there can damn it with fainter praise than 'Well.' They need to get the word out, pack those empty seats with paying butts. That reminds me."

The partitioned nook reserved for comedian Chuck Ramsey had a chair, mirror, and table, the latter of which was cluttered with household supplies lugged over from Logan Starport. Digging through spare diapers, pre-packaged snacks, and kids' toys, he located his datapad. The model was a few years past its prime, but it still took comms and had a quiet mode.

Flicking through menus, Chuck found what he was looking for.

FROM: Tru Fine Astrogation Service & Repair

RE: Star-Drive on RADIOCITY

Mr. Ramsey,

We took a look at that star-drive of yours. Mechanicals were misaligned. Easy fix. 500T and you're good there. But the misalignment's fouled the magical interface. Need a wizard for that. The guy we use charges 3,750T for a system this size. Need a confirm and 50 percent down to begin work.

Bing Cheedle, owner

Chuck held the datapad at arm's length, squinting to see if he could read any different words on the screen. He took another quick sip of his beer and tried again. No luck. Same screw job.

Shaking his head, he held up a warding finger to keep Becky from following him and made his way to the side exit of the theater.

The streets of Boston Prime were pristine. Buildings gleamed silver. The permacrete roads didn't bear so much as a crack or a scuff. Pedestrian and vehicular traffic flowed with purpose as upscale Earthlings buzzed about their important lives. Even the side alley where Chuck found himself on a short flight of steps was nicer than most colonies he'd visited.

In the relative quiet, Chuck placed a voice comm to his mechanic.

"*Yo, Bing here.*"

"Bing, you're killing me here."

"*Oh, it's you, Ramsey. Tough break on the wizard stuff.*"

"Who've you got realigning my star-drive? Houdini? Euclid? I'm not sure I can get 4,000T in salvage for the whole ship."

"*Not with a busted star-drive. Prolly not. Look, I know you're an offworlder—*"

"I'm from Chicago Prime!"

"*But this is what quality repair work costs Earthside these days.*"

Chuck paced the alley, running his fingers through his hair. This was a disaster. Earth was a black hole for terras, and this gig was only supposed to last a couple weeks. Laying ions as soon as he got paid was the only chance he had of turning a profit on this trip. If they didn't get offworld soon, Chuck might be forced to do the unthinkable...

Get a real job.

"Bing, lemme level with you. I don't have that kind of cash, digital *or* hardcoin. Don't you have another wizard, you know, someone who might owe you a favor?"

"*If I did, I wouldn't be charging* you *any less. Besides, those Convo boys don't break the rules. They got it too cushy taking guild rates.*"

Chuck wished *he* could pull in 3,000 terras for what amounted to probably half an hour's work. But he wasn't giving up yet.

"What about student wizards? There's a whole university full of them across town."

"Booked solid. They got a whole program. And they charge just as much. Listen, you got working engines and plenty of fuel. You're welcome to shop around for a better deal. No hard feelings."

"'Course," Chuck muttered as he ended the comm. When he slumped back against the wall of the theater, he couldn't help noticing Becky lurking in the doorway, little Rhiannon balanced on her hip. "How much you hear?"

"No scams," came her reply.

"But—"

"No scams." Becky ducked her head back inside the theater to check for eavesdroppers. "You hear me loud and clear, Charles Ramsey, this is Earth. Some of the stuff that flies out there will get you in real trouble here. You dig?"

Chuck opened his mouth to object. Then he caught The Look. This topic wasn't open to negotiation. There would be no Long Lost Loan, no Pawn Shop Swap, no Asteroid Investment this time.

With a sigh, he shook his head. "I dig it. We'll find a way off Earth. We just need to make some legit scratch on the side. Any ideas?"

Mordecai reached his grandparents' home after an energetic trek across the vacant quadrangle of Harvard. It was dark, but the starlight shone around the vacant black of a new moon. A night for new beginnings. He hated it when celestial events conspired to lend the appearance of omen, yet tonight it was difficult to deny the coincidence.

Relatives lounged in easy chairs and lay on couches, keeping a macabre vigil for the death of a man half of them couldn't stand and many of the rest barely knew. If not for Mordecai's wanton disregard for the accustomed quietude of the hour, most might have still been asleep as he blew past them.

Harald caught him in the hall outside Nebuchadnezzar's door. "There you are! We sent Gilly to the house, but you weren't there. He's locked himself inside and won't see anyone."

"I was working," Mordecai grumbled. "What's the problem? If he wants privacy, let him have it."

"He didn't eat anything since lunch. We're not all out here to let him die alone in there."

Scratching the stubble along his jawline, Mordecai realized how disheveled he must appear. "What'd he have for lunch?"

"Ham and Gouda sandwich with sardines and mustard."

Mordecai took the news with a grim nod. "Not my cup of oolong, but if that's what he wants for a last meal..."

"This is no time for joking. This is your department; get that door open so we can make sure he's OK."

"My department?" Mordecai arched an eyebrow.

"Yes. He's enspelled it with his own life force. None of us can think of a way to disable the wardings without killing him."

Rolling his eyes, Mordecai stepped past his great-uncle and knocked. "Granddad, you alive in there?"

The response came back muffled. "No thanks to these ghouls! Dust aside the Visigoths at my gates and get in here, my boy."

With a shrug that teetered on the socially acceptable

borderline between apologetic and gloating, Mordecai stared Harald back out of the way and let himself in. There was no resistance, either mystical or familial.

The ward sealed behind him.

Nebuchadnezzar sat up in bed looking brittle as a stale cracker but grinning a burglar's smile. "You read it. I can see it in you."

"You *asshole*!" Mordecai stalked across the room. "Did you have any idea what that book would do to me?"

"I had some notions. I didn't dare let another wizard try reading it after the two techies I exposed to it died in madness."

"You killed two people with that book?" Mordecai curled his fingers into claws, ready to strangle the last few hours of life out of that smug old carcass.

"Condemned criminals. I had a deal worked out with one of those fiddly secret Earth Parliament agencies. I forget which. Acronym. Lots of letters." He waved a bony hand. "But that's not important right now. You have to know why I wanted you to read it."

"I do." The book contained mysteries and toolsets, some so open-ended it might take him years to unpack it all. However, among the nebulous arts there were other, more blatant uses of the book's power.

"Hop to it, then. I'm ready."

Mordecai shook his head. "I don't get it. You'll *still* be dead."

"Am I a rack of bones wrapped in meat or a collection of thoughts, memories, emotions?"

"Both."

Nebuchadnezzar cackled. "That's scientist talk. This meat's rotting off the bone as we speak, but my mind's as hale as ever. I'm not done. Not quietly. Not in full possession of my faculties. Those *minions* out in the hall couldn't get in here."

Mordecai snorted.

"Oh. I know *you* could've. That's why I'm hitching my wagon to your star."

"Why not just go be with Isadora?" Mordecai swallowed, mouth gone dry. He didn't know quite what he believed, but his grandmother had seemed at peace when she passed.

"And risk that it's all a scam? What do I look like? A sucker? Isadora's mind had softened in her last years. That's how it's supposed to work. Senility is a gift so we don't see the cliff coming with no way to stop the avalanche we're riding toward oblivion."

"There won't be any hiding the evidence... unless I cremate you maybe." Of all the conversations he never expected to be having, planning the desecration of his grandfather's body—with his grandfather, no less—hadn't even found its way to the list.

"Way ahead of you. I *studied* that book, remember?"

"You're not letting me forget."

"You won't have to steal my mind. I'll come willingly—no, I'll *help*, even."

Nebuchadnezzar scooted down and lay beneath the covers. Mordecai stood over his grandfather's soon-to-be-corpse.

There was an ancient saying, a bit of advice handed down to children across the galaxy: "Never look a strange wizard in the eye." As dusty old bromides went, it was fairly practical. Most mental magics gained in power exponentially with direct eye contact.

Wizards as formidable as Mordecai and Nebuchadnezzar grew accustomed to ignoring that guideline and letting other people look away. Among their few peers, looking one another in the nose or mouth when conversing was the norm.

When those two pairs of eyes met, a storm unleashed. A maelstrom of every thought and feeling, all the memory, personality, and essence of Nebuchadnezzar The Brown passed to his grandson in an instant.

Blackness.

A void.

Endless.

Nebuchadnezzar stood a few feet away, dressed in the formal robes he'd have worn if he still held the title Guardian of the Plundered Tomes. Mordecai, identically attired, gaped.

Stretching and twisting through a few basic calisthenics, Nebuchadnezzar grinned like a madman. "Haha! Best I've felt since I was a lad. Thinker's all here."

"But nothing else is," Mordecai pointed out. "Is this what you were hoping for?"

"You shouldn't have done it," Mordecai replied. This was another Mordecai, indistinguishable in dress or appearance. He approached walking as if the void had an invisible floor.

Nebuchadnezzar swiveled his neck, looking from one to the other. "Two of you? Egad, what's going on here?"

The second Mordecai didn't slow his approach as he raised an accusing finger. "This copy of me is a monster. I'm the real Mordecai The Brown. Help me subdue him."

The original—as best he knew—Mordecai turned to his grandfather. "This is how you know I'm the real one." With a snap of his fingers, the doppelganger burst into flame, screaming as he flailed in a vain attempt to extinguish Promethean Fire. When the inferno died out, the dust swirled back into the nothingness from which it came.

"Ahh, so magic *does* work in here," Nebuchadnezzar observed sagely. "Excellent."

With a wave of his grandfather's hand, a grassy field appeared. As the old man flopped backward, a wooden park bench of a sort endemic to Boston Common appeared to catch him.

"Interesting," Mordecai said as he watched his grandfather create pigeons, then a small paper sack full of breadcrumbs.

"I'll be fine until you get back, my boy. Right as sunshine." With a snap, a sky appeared above them, casting noontime shadows. "You should get back and start consoling all the mourners."

Mordecai closed his eyes tight. When he opened them, he was standing over his grandfather's lifeless body. Yesterday, he'd have called it his mortal remains; now it seemed more like a hermit crab's discarded shell.

Not wanting to linger, he broke the old man's ward and opened the door.

Harald was the first to greet him. Nancy and the rest of the family who'd been awake crowded behind him.

"Nebuchadnezzar The Brown is dead," Mordecai pronounced.

"Dead?" Harald echoed incredulously. "You let him die without letting the rest of us—"

Mordecai snapped a hand up to cut him off. "His final words were for me alone. Guardian to Guardian. I will not repeat them until it's my own time to pass, when I will impart them to my successor."

With that, he retrieved Nancy and led her out of the house. A swarm of confused, grieving family flooded in the other direction.

Sunrises and sunsets took turns encircling Earth, and life returned to normal in Boston Prime. Nebuchadnezzar had been laid to rest in a solemn ceremony attended by the most important wizards on Earth. Few had shed tears. Wizards wore black often enough that mourning and daily fashion intermingled seamlessly.

Today, on a glorious sunny morning, Nancy Brown turned her attention to the younger generation. Cassandra and Cedric were of a precious age, cherubic and innocent, a phase that would pass all too soon. She swore not to miss a moment of it that could be helped. The grassy playground of Damon Square, just a few blocks from their home, was closed to the public. Cassie enjoyed a swing set, competing with the children of other wizards to see who could swing highest. Cedric enjoyed the sandbox, using precocious magic to collect piles into hills and mountains—a budding terramancer Nancy told herself, even though it was vain to project such high aspirations onto a four-year-old.

Nancy sipped her morning coffee, trying to capture the contentment she should be feeling.

It was the fault of neither bean nor brewer that the beverage was falling short of its duty. Her shoulders and neck were knotted and tense. While her eyes rested on her children, her mind wandered to her husband.

There had never been ease in the Grand Council since Mort's admission to the group. Nepotism, they said. Unfit, others claimed. Mort had shoved their complaints back into their smug, complacent faces. He was the best Guardian in centuries. Yet still, work plagued him.

Oh, Mort wouldn't let on knowingly. He probably even

thought he was fooling her. But this library census had been bothering him. Paperwork. Bertram and his cronies couldn't damn Mort on his merits, so they were tunneling beneath his feet with quills in lieu of shovels. Nancy was certain they were going to find some fault with his stewardship of the library, even though his real responsibilities lay outside the building.

Mort delivered fiery justice to dark wizards in the manner of the ancient gods, carrying on the tradition of Asaruludu, Uriel, and Surtr. Who were they to blame him for the bookkeeping?

It'll all be fine, she told herself. Mort was a thousand kinds of clever and bent the universe to his will like no wizard Nancy had ever met—not even dear old Nebuchadnezzar, the crusty curmudgeon. *Mort'll beat their dirty tricks.*

"Mrs. Brown?" a voice called from behind her.

Nancy turned in her bench seat to find a young man in the light gray uniform of the Convocation Technical Liaison's Office. "Yes. I'm Nancy Brown."

The young man handed her a datapad. "You've got a text comm. I've taken the liberty of opening it for you."

Nancy accepted with a gracious smile. "Thank you."

The liaison stood by like a bellhop awaiting a tip as she perused the document.

Dear arts patron,

Thank you for your purchase of two tickets for A Night of Laughter on Friday, September 30th. As a special bonus for valued guests, we're offering a limited number of backstage passes to meet Early Data comedian and entertainer extraordinaire Chuck Ramsey. Mr. Ramsey will be available for half an hour after final curtain for chatting, flatpics, and autographs. Act now. Tickets are on a first come, first serve basis.

We look forward to seeing you in person.

"How lovely," Nancy remarked. "Personalized thank you notes. I hadn't realized how considerate scientific sorts could be." She handed back the datapad. "Be a dear and buy those tickets before they're gone."

The liaison fiddled with the device briefly. "They're charging—"

"Tut-tut-tut," Nancy cut in. "It's a gift. I don't want to hear the price." Her own assistant would never have bothered her over terras spent on a show. In fact, Alexandretta hadn't when booking the show in the first place.

"They're not accepting Convocation credit," the liaison added apologetically.

Nancy blinked. With a flick of her finger, the device leapt from the young man's hand and flew into hers. She caught it smartly and squinted at the screen. It flickered briefly in protest of its magical handling but recovered in short order. Most of the workings of such devices eluded her, but someone once mentioned that a datapad screen was like a piece of parchment trapped under glass. Using her finger, she slid the paper around until she found the legalistic terms couched at the bottom.

"Cash only? In Boston? At a theater older than space travel?"

"Sorry, ma'am."

With a huff, she returned the device. "Make it happen."

"Ma'am?"

She looked him up and down. "You're more than two legs and a mouthful of polite excuses, I presume?" The liaison nodded. "Then figure it out. Your office has access to my digital money. Spend some of it. Pay yourself an appropriate fee. Scoot! Those tickets might be gone soon."

Once the tech helper had departed, Nancy returned to her coffee and spectating her children at play. Cassie had commandeered a horse on the merry-go-round. Cedric's sandbox now boasted a whimsical castle reminiscent of his Wax-i-Rod renderings.

The two of them were going to be fine. They had natural talent, minds sharp as vipers' fangs, and the Brown family name.

Mort had to contend with politicians.

Sitting with her ankles crossed atop the dining table in the *Radio City*, Becky Ramsey browsed the latest Earth gossip on the omni. She shared the datapad with Brad, but he was busy watching Blasterstar Launch Team on the holo-projector. Nothing took the mind off your own troubles like reading the ridiculous problems of the rich and famous.

Guy Miguel and Ananda Fiorina's divorce was hung up on custody of a parakeet.

Relatives of Esther Yamakura claimed her husband had her cloned to keep them from inheriting the house.

Acclaimed chef Brewster Barmy was being roasted for poaching his sesame kale sauce from an old tesud folk recipe.

An alert popped up. Becky had a text comm. It was a reminder that she needed to log out of her personal account before handing the datapad back to Brad, but it also came with a bonus: terras.

"Chuck!" she shouted over the din of zooming spaceships and explosions taking place in the middle of the ship's living room. "Come see this!"

Practically unnoticed amid the holographic din, the sound

of a shower ceased. A moment later, dripping and wrapped in a towel, Chuck stepped out and crossed the living room, dodging an asteroid field of toys and the children playing with them on the floor. "We win the lottery or something?"

Becky grinned as she handed him the datapad. "This outta sight, or what?"

Chuck studied it for a moment, hair dripping onto the screen. "What kind of square is willing to pay to talk to me after the show?"

"The kind who pays in hard, plastic Earth-cookies with pictures of The Pantheon on them."

"Can't knock untraceable terras. How'd you get an Earthling to pay hardcoin?"

"You say that like you're not from here."

Chuck shook his hair, intentionally spraying droplets in all directions. Mike and Rhiannon, caught in the brief rain shower, giggled and sought shelter. "Nah. Born here and from here aren't the same thing. But if being born here taught me one thing, it's that Earthlings think anyone who deals in physical money is shady."

"Except wizards."

Chuck stuck a finger in his ear, twisted it around, then asked, "Did you say wizards?"

"We're ten meters from Convocation HQ. Why not wizards?"

"Are we insured against magical mishaps?"

Becky pursed her lips and scowled. "No..."

"Could we afford to—?"

"No scams!" She slapped him gently with the datapad and had the satisfaction of seeing him cringe as if she'd hit him with a golf club.

"OK. OK. Got it. Chill out."

"You be on your best behavior, Comedian Chuck Ramsey. If we can get hip to the wizard groove, they'll start telling their rich wizard friends and we can make enough scratch to blow this overpriced museum of a planet. Maybe even snag a favor to fix the star-drive on the cheap."

Chuck's grin spread slowly as he nodded along. "Far out. Great work, babe."

"Now go crash for a couple so you're fresh for tonight's show."

Eleven wizards bore down the weight of their ancient eyes upon the twelfth of their number. Mordecai The Brown swept his gaze around the vast table's circumference, seeking pity or sympathy in any of his fellows. He found nothing but scorn. The air hung heavy and still in the Convocation's Grand Council Chamber, the echoic reaches of the vaulted stone ceiling finding no sound worth magnifying or repeating. Sunlight poured through stained glass windows depicting Merlin bestowing Excalibur upon Arthur, St. George slaying the last dragon on Earth, and the sinking of Atlantis. The beams caught motes of dust in their trails and made time flow like cold honey. Everyone waited for him.

"I can offer no explanation," Mordecai replied. He sat with his arms resting on the table's timeworn stone surface, hands tucked within opposing sleeves, wet with perspiration. There was no wizard among them who was his junior, but he was not the least of their number. He held his chin high and fought to keep his breathing steady.

"Do you dispute the library census?" Bertram Hancock, the holder of the First Chair, asked, shaking a leather-bound ledger. It had a listing of every book in the Convocation's libraries, from the memoirs of long-dead wizards to mundane works of history and mathematics. It also contained listings of the Plundered Tomes. A few were harmless, but most were forbidden to even open, for the dark magics described therein contained the roots of the malevolence that had spawned those ancient enemies.

One of those tomes was missing.

As Guardian of the Plundered Tomes, responsibility fell to Mordecai. "I've verified it myself. The census seems to be correct."

"No one gets in or out of the vault without your knowledge," said Pao Wenling, the holder of the Third Seat and Chief Inquisitor of the Convocation. Her statement had the vague sense of a question lingering about its edges but stung as an accusation.

"I had always presumed so," Mordecai said, "but I admit the possibility that someone has."

"You're couching your words carefully, Mordecai," Bertram said, tapping the fingertips of one hand on the census ledger. It wasn't as if Mordecai was going to forget that it was there.

"Too carefully, perhaps," Wenling agreed. The rest of the wizards looked on, mere spectators. They were there to witness, to add gravitas... possibly to lend aid in overpowering Mordecai if things turned impolite.

He searched for a sign that anyone disagreed with Wenling's assessment. In the Fourth Chair, Ronald Sternenlicht wouldn't meet his eye. In the Sixth Chair, his cousin Ezekiel knit his brow and tried to make Mordecai look elsewhere. Diane Smythe, in the Eleventh Chair, spared him the twitch of a smile, and that was the best he was going to get.

"So what is it, then?" Mordecai snapped. "Vague accusations? Discrepant reports? A bloody book is missing, and we all know it. What are you more interested in, having someone's eyes out for reading a forbidden tome, burning me at the stake for letting him, or finding the damned thing and getting it back?"

In the silence that followed, Mordecai began to worry that perhaps retrieval of the book was not their highest priority. Options swirled in his mind, contingencies for avoiding a stake-burning that would only be figurative in the sense that outdoor human barbecues were illegal on Earth. Wenling and Bertram exchanged a look across the table. Mordecai held his next breath, wondering how many more like it were left in him.

"Very well," Bertram said. "As the guardian responsible, I charge you with finding and returning the book, and dealing with the perpetrator of the theft. You have three days. Come sunset Monday, we will have either the book or your resignation."

"Thank you," Mordecai said. "Three days will be plenty." Plenty of time to get away.

"I will conduct my own investigation as well," Wenling said. She graced Mordecai with a smile that said she was trying to help, but the look in her eyes made him suspect she would be investigating him.

"Well, then," Bertram said. "There is much to be done. I see no reason to detain either of you. Council is adjourned."

The air outside Convocation Hall was crisp and fresh with the scent of autumn leaves. Boston Prime was one of the few urban areas left on Earth with tree-lined parks, thanks to the wizards who paid exorbitant taxes for land with nothing but dirt and flora. Mordecai savored the walk back to the churning bustle of the surrounding city.

Nancy was waiting for him on a bench, watching the sunset over the cityscape. She turned at the sound of his footsteps. "Hey there, handsome," she called out as he approached. She was dressed for the weather in a baggy wool sweater and her hair pulled up under a matching knit hat.

Mordecai reached down and offered his hand to help her up, and she kissed him as he pulled her close. "Let's get out of here," he said.

"Ooh, that doesn't sound good," Nancy said, falling into step beside Mordecai and taking three steps for every two of his. "I'd hoped you'd clear everything up in there."

"Didn't shake out like that," he replied. "They gave me three days. I've got to find the book and bring it back."

"Oh," Nancy replied. Then after a moment's pause, "I guess you'll have your hands full this evening."

Mordecai could read her like a written page. "What'd you have planned?"

"The kids are staying with your father for the evening. I got us tickets to a show... it was a birthday surprise."

Mordecai snorted. "It's not my birthday. But you knew that."

Nancy's smile cut through the knot of worry binding his guts. "I can't surprise you on your birthday anymore. You get all defensive and paranoid, and I wanted a real surprise this year. But now..."

"Aw, hell," Mordecai said, kicking a twig off the flagstone path. "The damn book can wait. Where we going?"

"You sure, Mort?"

"Absolutely." Since his investigation was going to be a farce, losing time wasn't a concern. "Anything to clear my head. Just... well, it's not some singing show, is it?"

She laughed. "Yes, Mort. I'm dragging you to the opera. I always torment you for your birthday, don't I?" When he raised an eyebrow in mock alarm, she relented. "It's a comedy show, as hokey and old-fashioned as I could find."

"More like it..." he muttered.

They passed under a wrought iron archway that allowed passage through the ivy-laden red brick wall surrounding the Convocation grounds. Beyond the reach of the subtle magic that kept the peace and solitude of the wizards undisturbed, the modern world rushed in. The air swarmed with the repulsor lights of uncountable cars, freighters, and patrol ships. Luna was visible in the sky above, the blue-green surface of Earth's only moon, half full.

At the sidewalk's edge, a line of taxis bobbed, waiting for passengers. Mort picked one at random and opened the door for Nancy.

"Good evening," the driver said. "Fifty terras, anywhere in the city. One hundred for the region. Five for anywhere planetside. I don't do off-Earth. Where are we heading tonight?" The spiel was well rehearsed and fluid, with no polite point for a passenger to break in with a question.

Mordecai looked to Nancy since he had no idea where they were going. "Orpheum Theater," she said to the driver. "See? Oldest theater in Boston Prime. Plus, we don't even cross an ocean tonight." For a notorious homebody like Mordecai, being stuck in a science-powered vessel for half an hour or more always fouled his mood.

"Excellent, ma'am," the driver said. "Fifty terras, digital or hardcoin?"

Mordecai held up the palm of one hand and a symbol appeared between his outstretched fingers, the stroke of lightning crashing through the letter C. The symbol of the Convocation. "Convocation's tab," he said gravely. It always helped to keep a serious tone when acting the part of a wizard, lest regular folk get the impression that wizards were people just like them.

The driver straightened in his seat, his easy friendliness turned formal in an instant. "Yes, sir!"

Mordecai and Nancy tucked their hands into opposing sleeves and settled in for the ride. It was a gesture more than anything—reassurance to the driver that they would work no magic. Few wizards were foolish enough to try spells while aboard a moving vehicle, but it never hurt to show good faith and good manners.

The Orpheum Theater had a pleasant weight of age. It was almost seven hundred years old, and Mordecai imagined that he could feel the ghosts of performers long dead watching over the place. It had been refurbished a number of times, but always with an eye toward preservation rather than modernization. A wizard's critical eye could pick up a holo-projector here, or a security scanner there, but looking past those, it was easy to let the mind drift back to a simpler era. The seats were upholstered patterned cotton, the curtains red velvet. The ionic columns were a throwback to ancient Greek times even when the place was new, and the vaulted ceiling hearkened to Renaissance architecture.

Nancy caught him gawking. "You like it?"

"How is it that you've never taken me here?"

"You're the most curmudgeonly thirty-two-year-old anyone's ever been," she replied. "If I'd have known old theaters would pique your interest, I'd have tried them years ago."

Mordecai said nothing in reply. He wanted to tell her that she could take him wherever she liked. That anywhere would be fine. That she was all he needed to be happy wherever he was. But he didn't trust himself. He risked ruining the night if he let slip how desperate he was. There were three days, and Convocation be damned, he was going to milk them for all their worth.

Their seats were mezzanine level, front and center, looking down at the stage from so close that he could loft a paper starship down at the performers. As the audience filled the theater, ambient music rose from unseen sources. "What's this?" Mort asked, unfamiliar with the tunes.

Nancy pressed a program into his hands. "It's a twentieth-century themed show. The music is period. To set a mood, I imagine." It was twangy and fuzzy, with a pronounced rhythm and up-tempo beat. There were lyrics, but Mordecai would be damned if he could tell what language they were. It sounded Earth-like. After a moment's devoted listening, he picked out a word here or there and realized that the whole bloody thing was sung in English, but with the most horrid enunciation imagined.

As the crowd packed in around him, Mordecai grew tense. Something felt wrong, but he couldn't place it. Nancy put a hand on his knee. "What's eating you? Did that hearing go worse than you're letting on?"

"Yes," Mordecai murmured. "Much. Someone's following us. I can't place them, but feel the air. Someone's steadying the room, down in the lower seats." It would have been a hard concept to explain to a non-wizard, but Nancy's arcane powers were nearly as strong as his. A wizard not working magic kept an area of the universe stable around himself. The laws of physics did not bend so easily when someone else believed strongly in the status quo. A subtle mind could sniff out when such supernatural stability was in play.

"Mort..." Nancy said. "Why are you being followed?" Damn. He had let too much slip.

He patted her hand where it rested on his knee. "Nothing that will spoil a show," he assured her.

When the show began, headlining comedian Chuck Ramsey came onto the stage, smiling and waving, an old-fashioned handheld microphone clutched in one hand. "Good evening, everyone! Great to be back on Earth. It's been so long, I feel like a xeno on my own planet. Did you folks evolve while I was gone? Everyone seems to have more hair than me. I've been touring the borderlands, and let me tell you, the food is nothing like what we get here on Earth. I mean, where else can you get a synth-meat hamburger with chemically simulated cheese and bacon, soy-byproduct fries, and medical treatment for it the same night...?" The audience laughed, and Mordecai chuckled along with them. The comedian was making fun of modern Earth. It was stupid, childish humor, and it was funny.

Chuck Ramsey introduced several other comedians for short bits, then put on an hour-long show himself. Topics ranged all over the spectrum. Why couldn't Earth stop itself from invading smaller planets? Poor service on interstellar transports. Child-rearing tips and the best threats to use on children, as learned from his father. Seven words that you couldn't say on Mars. How Luna was terraformed just to get all the lunatics to move there. He even went back to his burger joke from earlier and expounded on how the iconic meal differed throughout Earth-controlled space.

Mordecai couldn't get enough. It was low-science, low-complexity humor filled with an overriding folksy wisdom that felt timeless. He laughed along with Nancy and thanked his lucky stars that he had a wife who understood him. It took his mind off his troubles, at least for a little while. After Chuck Ramsey took his bows and the spotlight disappeared, house lights came up. It was just a historic building in the theater district of Boston Prime again. Mordecai stood and let out a long, wistful breath that carried that momentary sense of wonderment along with it.

"You seemed to enjoy yourself," Nancy said. "See what happens when you leave the house to go someplace besides work?"

Mordecai nodded. "I needed that. How would you fancy a walk home? It can't be more than a couple miles."

"Actually, I've got one more surprise for you," Nancy replied. "But I wanted to see how you liked the show first. I got us backstage clearance."

Mordecai raised an eyebrow. "You know, I wouldn't half mind meeting that Ramsey fellow."

The dressing room for the comedy show wasn't quite what Mordecai had envisioned. He had assumed it would be a bustle of production assistants and comedians half-changed between stage attire and what they wore about town. What he hadn't anticipated was a childcare center. The comedians were in the anticipated state of dishabille, but the rest was a mass of yowling children and the wives and husbands trying to wrangle them.

"You must be the Browns," Chuck Ramsey greeted them, sticking a hand out for Mort to shake. He had removed his suit coat and tie, and his brow glistened with sweat from standing under the house lights for an hour. "Wizards, I hear. I always wondered what sort of nutter paid extra to meet me. Guess now I know."

Mordecai couldn't take offense with Chuck's rough assessment. In truth, he had always found that he and his fellow wizards were proper nutters. "I'm Mordecai, but anyone without a stick up his ass calls me Mort. This is my wife, Nancy."

"Pleased to meet you," Chuck said. He twisted around and checked over his shoulder in the dressing room mirror. "Mort." He winked at Nancy, who giggled. Mordecai couldn't even fault the man's flirtation—he was a showman, after all. It came with the territory. "This is my wife, Becky. My two youngest, Mike and Rhiannon. My oldest is around here somewhere, too."

"Hi!" A voice caught Mordecai's attention from behind. "My name's Bradley Carlin Ramsey. Pleased to meet you, Mort." The boy was eleven, possibly twelve years old, with an unruly mop of hair and bright green eyes that looked like they were aimed at something. Most children had eyes that wandered—even his own were prone to inattention—and few gave a thought to looking square at an adult. The boy stuck a hand out in imitation of his father. The young Ramsey gritted his teeth as he squeezed, but it was a boy's handshake, however much he tried.

Mordecai gave the boy a fearsome mock scowl. "Shouldn't that be Mr. Brown?"

The boy shook his head. "I don't have a stick up my..." He glanced to his mother, whose face bore a more threatening scowl. "...bum."

Mordecai tousled the boy's hair and turned his attention back to the father. "So, what gets a man into comedy?" he asked and eyed the backstage setup critically. "Doesn't look like it's a path to riches."

"Mort!" Nancy exclaimed.

Chuck laughed. "Don't worry, Nancy. Gotta have a thick skin in this business. Besides, Mort's right. It keeps fuel in the engines and food on the table. All you need, really. I get to set my own hours and captain my own ship... see the galaxy on my own terms. You can join the navy and see the before-and-after from a bomber's window, but I like my way better. Plus, I can have my family along."

"You own your own ship?" Mordecai asked. His opinion of the man rose. "Must make things easier for your line of work."

"Can't break even these days paying other people to fly you around planet to planet, gig to gig," Chuck replied. "Just not enough money in it. Worst I gotta pay now is fuel costs and star-drive repairs. Damn things break down every five drops or so."

"Magic and science shouldn't mix," Mordecai replied. "Those things are fundamentally flawed. Constantly at odds. There's a whole legion of drooling half-wizards employed in fixing them. That ought to tell folks all they need to know."

"Mort, don't go on one of your tirades," Nancy scolded him.

Chuck waved a lazy hand. "Naw, let him go. Comedians are the philosophers of their time. Meeting people from all walks of life and getting snips of the galaxy through their eyes, that's what it's all about. Maybe one day I'll do a star-drive mechanic bit."

"You're... going to make a comedy skit based on me? On what I just said?" Mordecai asked. He turned to Nancy. "We didn't agree to any of that, did we?"

"Whoa, whoa, big guy," Chuck said, holding up his hands. He grabbed a bottle from the dressing room table and popped it open. "You don't want to be in a joke, fine. Can I interest you in a bottle of Chateau Noir '40?"

Mordecai eyed the bottle. "I assume that's this year's vintage and not some number of hundreds of years old."

Chuck grinned. "Stuff's not even old enough to walk."

"Got any beer?" Mordecai asked.

"I'll have a glass," Nancy replied politely.

"Becky, we got anything like a glass?" Chuck asked over his shoulder.

"Spill-proofs for Rhiannon," Becky suggested.

Chuck dug into a cooler and tossed Mordecai an Earth's Preferred, the cheapest dishwater suds the planet exported.

"I didn't even know they sold this stuff on Earth," Mordecai said.

"They don't, far as I know," Chuck replied. "We always pick up extra when we're heading for Earth." He took a second can for himself.

"This is lovely," Nancy said, sipping newborn wine from a bright red plastic cup with a molded-in straw. She forced a smile.

Chuck shrugged. "Nothin's fancy in this life," he said. "But I wouldn't trade it for the world. I scrape by, raise my own kids, and don't have anyone looking over my shoulder all the time."

"You have quite the interesting life," Nancy said, and

Mordecai knew she was saying it just to be nice. For all the rough edges though, Mordecai could see the appeal.

Chuck's fingers cramped, and he shook them to loosen the muscles. The seven of diamonds lay accusingly on the floor beside the hat it missed. It wasn't alone. Half a deck of specialized metallic cards lay strewn around it. Three had managed to land inside.

Emitting a frustrated huff, Chuck bent down and scooped up the hat. Something had to be wrong with it. He flipped it over and gave a gentle shake. The cards remained plastered to the inside. The magnets were doing their job.

"Pshaw. This thing's just messing with me." He flung the hat to the floor, and several nearby cards slurped into it. "Sure, *now* you wanna catch 'em."

The opening of the living room door startled Chuck. His mind began a hasty inventory of anything that might be considered worth stealing. Then, remembering he was parked on Earth, he switched to taking stock of anything aboard the *Radio City* that might count as evidence.

"Hi, Dad," Bradley announced with an incline of his head as he breezed in. The casual obliviousness of prepubescence never ceased to amaze Chuck.

"What're you doing back? What happened to the zoo?"

Bradley shrugged. "Zoos are kinda scratchy, aren't they? Rather chill with you."

"Mom wanted you to carry Rhi, didn't she?"

Flopping onto the couch, Bradley rolled his eyes. "I get it. Stroller rentals cost terras. But she's getting too heavy."

"Builds muscle," Chuck retorted, flexing a bicep and patting it.

"And she's always sticky."

Chuck nodded, unable to deny the point.

"Besides, I figured you must be up to something for Mom to want us out of the way."

Studiously, Chuck avoided glancing down at the trick hat on the floor. "'Course I'm up to something. But it's Earth, so there's not much 'something' to get up to."

"I want in."

Chuck broke out laughing. "C'mon, sport. Get real. How much you in the hole just hoofing it back here?" Becky would have taken the kids on public transit, but unaccompanied minors weren't eligible for family discounts.

"Nothing."

A likely story. Chuck openly scoffed. "Your old man wasn't born yesterday. This is Earth. There's a surcharge in the docking fees to pay for the fresh air."

"Hitched a ride."

"You *what*?"

"Chill out, Dad. I was careful."

Chuck folded his arms. "Oh yeah?"

"Caught up with a family leaving the zoo. Claimed I got separated from my parents."

"And they didn't take you to the security station?"

Bradley shook his head. "I told them I was supposed to meet them at Logan Starport if we got separated. 'That's the family emergency plan,' I told them. They bought it. And I knew they were already heading for Logan because they had the same rental stroller Mom refused to pay for when we were leaving."

Where was the hole in Bradley's plan? Chuck couldn't let

the kid think he already had all the answers before he hit puberty, otherwise Bradley would be even *more* insufferable during his teen years than he and Becky were already bracing for. "What if they were kidnappers?"

"You and Mom can't afford fuel rods. Maybe I'd be trading up."

It wasn't subtle when Bradley tried winding him up. Chuck ignored the obvious bait. "What if they were connected?"

"To the syndicates? I could be so lucky. I'd make a great gangster."

There wasn't much arguing that one. Chuck changed tactics. "What if they had a daughter about your age back on their ship? She didn't want to go to the zoo either. She wants to hold hands and dance to slow music."

"I can handle myself."

Chuck's eyes nearly fell out of their sockets.

Bradley grinned.

Wagging a finger, Chuck conceded his defeat. "You had me going there, kiddo. You start chasing after girls, and we gotta whole new curriculum to cover. Your old man knows a thing or two about—"

"Getting wrapped around Mom's finger."

"That too. But before your mom, your old man had a reputation as a ladies' man."

"I want in."

"On what?" Chuck demanded. He hated falling behind in a conversation, and Bradley was developing an annoying habit of taking shortcuts to get out ahead of him.

"Whatever you've got planned that Mom didn't make you come to the zoo with us."

What, indeed? In Chuck's version of events, there had

been a hushed argument before the kids woke up. She wanted the kids to glean a little Earth culture before they left and wanted to spend some of their star-drive fund to do it. Chuck wanted offworld as soon as sentiently possible; he'd put his foot down. Becky had refused to help raise additional funds until she got a say in spending them; Chuck had caved.

"Sure. I guess you've earned a piece of the action. You... uh... got any ideas of your own before we delve into my master plan?"

Eyes gleaming with avarice, Bradley practically nodded his head right off his spindly neck. "I was thinking about Mom's rules and how we could get around them."

"Oh, so today's one of those days that starts in a consonant."

"We need to find legitimate work..."

Chuck arched a skeptical eyebrow.

"But take a job from someone who's not."

Click. That was the piece of the puzzle Chuck was missing. "Not half bad, kid."

It took a little more than an hour. Chuck registered a corporation out of Telessel VI at a whopping cost of 8T. Bradley created fake accounts on ConsumerYak and left a variety of positive ratings. Chuck coached him on the innocuous phrases to pepper into his reviews.

"Super helpful and discreet."

"I hired Planetary Parcel Packers for a long-haul job, and it got done fast and flawlessly."

"They didn't ask a lot of questions. Just delivered my freight. Would hire again."

"I paid the expedite fee and never regretted it. Fastest delivery ever."

By the two-hour mark, they had their first client lined up.

Bradley kept his mouth shut as the sucker showed up and dumped a grav sled loaded with sealed crates marked TOOTH SOAP at their landing pad. Best of all, Chuck collected 1,800T up front for the privilege.

"Sure. Orion. Day after tomorrow. No problem at all." They'd shaken hands, and the sucker had zipped off to whatever part of Earth he'd come from.

Bradley looked up at him when the guy was out of range of possibly hearing. "What now? Can we make it to Orion in two days?"

"Not until we get our star-drive fixed."

"That won't cover the repairs."

Chuck snickered. "Yeah. But that guy gave us more than 1,800T." He shared a knowing glance with his son.

Then, both turned in unison to gaze at the stacks of crates.

Morning had neither crept up nor sprung upon him, but Mordecai was awake before the dawn. Nancy still clung to her slumber, wrung out to exhaustion the night before by their invigorating walk home in the small hours and the lovemaking that followed. The house was quiet with the children asleep. Too quiet. This wasn't how he wanted to remember it. He wanted to bump into Cedric's blocks levitating in the hall, or catch Cassandra trying to curdle the milk in his cereal without him noticing.

"What's wrong, grumpyface?" Nancy mumbled half into her pillow. She had one heavy-lidded eye focused on him.

It was time. The darkened hours alone with his thoughts had assembled the disparate pieces of a plan that had floated within the twisted halls of his mind. He had to tell Nancy. "I have to go," he said.

"Go where? It's Saturday, Mort," Nancy replied. "Sleep in."

"I'm not going to find that book," Mordecai replied. "Neither is Wenling."

"Hmm?"

He threw off the blankets and stood. Warmth from the magically heated oak floor seeped into his cold feet, soothing them as he walked to the bureau. "Last night was wonderful, but I can't afford to lose more time. Those three days were a reprieve, a farewell."

"Mort, you're scaring me," Nancy said, sitting up in bed and pulling the blanket to cover herself.

"I'm sorry," Mordecai replied. "But you might need to be, at least for a little while. But be scared for me, not yourself. After I've left, go stay with my father until things cool down. My father won't let anything happen to you or the kids. You're innocent in all of this."

"You lost a book," Nancy said. "Even if it never gets found, what's the worst they're going to do, make you resign? You're over—"

"It was me," Mordecai snapped. "Everyone who's ever held my post sticks their nose in the forbidden texts once in a while. It's no big deal. Builds character, resisting those nasty old words left by dead wizards of old. But this one got to me. I read every word of it, and it still haunts me. I burned it."

"You didn't..."

"I've covered my tracks. Fudged a few records. I thought I might get past the book census, but those buggers under Kramer were thorough. I don't know how long I have before the Convocation figures it out, but if I'm here when they do,

I'm done for." Mordecai stuffed garment after garment into a knapsack, long after it should have been stuffed to overflowing.

"This is crazy, Mort. Go see your father. There's no need for this to get blown out of proportion."

"My father?" Mordecai scoffed. "The great Alastair The Brown, defend a book-burner? Only three copies of that book ever existed, and the other two are lost. I've destroyed priceless history, and the only thing that might stop them reducing me to cinders is the fact that it carved its wicked words into my mind. I might be the last copy out there."

"What book was this, anyway?"

"I won't speak its title aloud. The less you know, the better." Mordecai scanned along his bookshelves, picking out a selection to shove into the pack with the rest of his travel supplies.

"So you're going to run away?" Nancy demanded, letting go of the blanket and folding her arms. "Abandon me and the children? Think this through, Mordecai The Brown."

"I have," Mordecai replied. "I was up all last night and for weeks since the census was announced. I've wondered what I'd do ever since I put that book to the flame. You had no part in this. You and the children will live with the shame of what I've done, and I'm sorry for that. But life will go on."

"And what am I supposed to tell Cedric and Cassie?" she asked. "That their father is a criminal on the run? How will they face up to their mistakes if you don't?"

"Well, if anyone is ever after them to carve the eyes out of their skulls to see what they've seen, I won't hold it against them if they tuck tail and run," Mordecai replied. He took his best staff made from ancient oak—from the days when Earthwood was still legal—and packed it away, along with his pendant of office.

"Good god, Mort. Really?"

"If I'm lucky, they wouldn't kill me in the process," Mordecai replied. He snorted. "Lucky..."

"But where will you go?" Nancy asked.

"If I told you, you'd only have to worry about letting it slip. There'll be hell enough to pay when you don't run straight to Bertram and tell him everything I've just said to you, but that I think my father can protect you from."

"How long will you be on the run?"

"I'll look for another copy of the tome," Mordecai said. It was a lie, but one Nancy needed to hear. He could have written the book from memory if he chose, but there was no way he could bring himself to recreate it. No, if he were to look for the other two copies, it would be to burn them as well. "If I can replace it, maybe I can gain a reprieve. Or maybe Bertram's successor won't be such a hard-ass, and I can get clemency. Until then though? I'll keep moving."

Nancy stood at the doorway as Mordecai crept into Cassandra's room. The soft glow of conjured fireflies kept the worst of the darkness at bay. She had been afraid of the dark once, and Mordecai had created them to make her feel safe. There had been hundreds at first, but night by night, Mordecai had reduced the fireflies in number until only a handful remained and Cassandra no longer feared the night. For her last birthday, she had asked for them back because they were pretty. As Mordecai navigated an obstacle course of scattered toys, he was thankful that he had obliged her.

He hadn't known Nancy at that age—they had met while both attending Oxford—but he had seen old pictures of her, and Cassandra was her time-lost twin, separated by a mere twenty-four years. His daughter slept heavily, worn ragged by a day spent horseback riding with her cousins. Tousled hair lay splayed across her pillow. A bruise darkened one cheek where Cedric had struck her with one of his alphabet blocks. Mordecai smiled—the simple, innocent dangers of childhood.

Without a word, he bent over the sleeping Cassandra and brushed the hair from her face. She stirred and rolled onto her side but didn't wake. Mordecai planted a gentle kiss on her forehead. He whispered, too softly for Nancy to hear him from the doorway. "My little angel. Mommy's going to need you to be strong and brave. Just remember I love you and want nothing more than for you to be happy and safe."

He kissed her once again and added a kiss for Nancy on his way out the door. By the light of the fireflies, he could see the wet streaks down her cheeks.

Cedric's room was simpler, kept tidy by the nanny. An arcane orb lit overhead at a gesture from Mordecai. The boy had outgrown his crib, but still slept in a tiny bed, low to the floor. Mordecai knelt beside his son's sleeping form. The blankets were thrown aside, and the sheets tangled themselves around Cedric's legs; even in sleep the active lad couldn't keep still for long. Family stories said that Mordecai had been the same way at that age.

Same as he had done with Cassandra, Mordecai kissed Cedric on the forehead. But he was no sleeping dragon like his sister; he was a watchdog. In an instant, Cedric's eyes were open. "What is it, Daddy?"

Mordecai swallowed past the lump in his throat. "I have to go away for a while, Ceddie. You'll have to be the man of the house while I'm gone."

Cedric rubbed one eye with his fist. "When are you coming back?"

"Not for a long time," Mordecai said. "But every time you ask how long, or even think to wonder, I'll be gone a little longer. Can you hold your tongue and still your thoughts about something you can't change?" It was a horrible thing to ask of a four-year-old. But Nancy would go mad with worry if persistent little Cedric badgered her about him.

"Yes, Daddy," Cedric replied. Despite the yawn in his voice, and despite his tender age, Mordecai knew he would remember. Cedric was brighter than fire, even laying aside fatherly bias.

"Good boy," Mort said, stroking his head. "Now go back to sleep. Tomorrow is a big day."

Cedric smiled sleepily. "Every day is a big day." Mordecai had taught him that one. But this time it was more true than usual. Tomorrow would be the day that Cedric lost his father. There was never any guarantee that a big day was a good one. It hurt in the pit of his stomach to know what was coming for the boy.

As soon as the door shut, Nancy collapsed against his chest, sobbing quietly. Mordecai just held her there, waiting. There were words brewing, he could tell. Best to let them steep until they were ready.

"Stay," Nancy said, her voice trembling.

"I wish I—"

"You can," she said. From within his embrace, she looked into his eyes, craning her neck as he towered over her. "You can beat this. You've got friends, connections. It'll be ugly, but—"

"No," Mordecai said. "I have nothing... nothing but a family I need to keep safe from this business. Those friends, those political allies of convenience? The wind has changed, and their sails are already set for it. Lie to the children, or trust them with the truth. You'll be able to judge which will be better for them, and I've got no right to a say. Just... never let them forget that I love them."

How long they stayed in each other's arms, Mordecai couldn't say. Forever would have been too little time. And then it was time for him to disappear.

Bing stood impassive. The only motion in his face involved the chewing of bite after bite of an extra-large hoagie from Isfearr Delicatessen. Chuck suspected that he only had until the end of that 30cm sandwich to make his case.

"Y'see, it's like this," he explained, trying his third different tactic since the conversation started, roughly eight bites ago. "If I get the star-drive fixed *today*, then I make the delivery early and get a bonus. That bonus more than covers the repairs plus my operating costs. We both win here. What am I missing?"

Bing paused, one cheek puffed out, then swallowed what was probably a bite not ready to go down just yet. "The part where you pay me before leaving Earth."

Chuck chewed the inside of his cheek a moment. "You know what? I'm gonna let you in on a little secret. You know what's in those crates?"

"That's another thing," Bing replied, nonplussed by the dangling offer. "I don't like seeing cargo in sealed, scan-resistant containers stacked next to a ship I'm working on."

Spreading his hands with a "so what?" gesture, Chuck replied, "This is Earth. There's no such thing as contraband here. The stars are painted in silver and the air itself is perfumed with saffron. I could see your point if I was shipping in stuff from Mars—"

"My sister-in-law's Martian."

"But if a local businessman wants to keep his proprietary business dealings private, who am I to run a Remmington Mk 2.3 scanner over them to check for anything worth making a fuss over?"

The faux indignation Bing had placed on display with that anemic crack about his brother's wife faded. In its place, embarrassment set in, marked by shifting of the mechanic's weight to hide the aforementioned scanner clipped to his belt. "Look. I don't care if you're due a half million terras on the far end of this cargo run you've got. I'm not a bank."

"I'm not asking for money. I'm looking for a working star-drive, and you *are* a mechanic." Chuck had checked the man's publicly available credentials, just to be sure.

"Look, Chuck. I like you. Family man. Own your own ship. But I got a policy: no loans to offworlders. And... no offense, but especially not to ones who talk *quite* so fast."

"*Moi*, talk fast? If I'm running a little loose at the lips, it's only because I've got a family to feed, a ship that needs repairs, and two days to cross a good chunk of the core."

With a sigh, Bing crumpled the wrapper his hoagie came in and stuffed it in a pocket, then leaned against the hull of the *Radio City*. "Chuck. You want some free advice?"

"Only kind I can afford..."

"You've got a star-drive that was never meant for a ship this size. Every drop, you're stressing the poor thing to its limit."

"Guy I got it from swore up and down it was top-of-the-line."

"Thirty years ago? Maybe. And for a ship two-thirds the tonnage." He thumped a fist against the ship's outer plating.

"But this thick boy needs something with more oomph. Stick to 1 or 2 AU, and maybe you can get by a couple more years without a complete failure. Otherwise..." He shrugged.

"But it manages just fine," Chuck protested.

"It's like a stuunji riding a burro."

Chuck blinked his utter lack of comprehension.

Scowling, Bing tried again. "A piggyback ride for a laaku?"

With a forced guffaw, Chuck reached back and tousled the hair of Bradley, who'd been lurking silently at the periphery of the conversation, learning from a master of his craft. "Aww, a grown laaku weighs less than my boy here."

There was a time-honored tradition of letting anyone you're negotiating with keep talking. The longer a mark danced around the hook, the more chances he had to get himself snagged. But this mechanic was starting to get on Chuck's nerves with his nonsense.

Extending an index and pinkie finger, Bing gave a twist of his wrist. "Other way around. The laaku is doing the carrying."

"But that would be... oh. That bad?"

Bing nodded.

"And you wouldn't do a family man like me a favor this once?"

The mechanic used his hips and pushed away from the hull. He stood a moment, jaw set, brow furrowed. A light smoke could have issued from the man's ears without surprising Chuck just then. "Nope."

Chuck offered a handshake as Bing headed off to do whatever it was he did when he wasn't crushing dreams. "Stick close. If I come up with the terras, you'll be the first to know."

Bing grunted something noncommittal as he accepted the handshake by reflex.

Bradley watched alongside his dad until the man was out of sight. "Guy's kind of an asshole, huh?"

"You know your mom doesn't like you talking like that."

"But she's not here and you do. And Bing's a galaxy-grade keester with a head sticking out. What do we do now?"

Sizing up the cargo, Chuck gave one of the crates a test-lift, finding it to be heavier than he had any intention of lugging aboard, let alone its numerous companions. Then he sized up his son and compared the two.

Not a chance the kid could budge these things.

"Go find my guitar."

"Your guitar? What for?"

"I'm gonna hire some guys to haul this all aboard, and after paying Earth rates for menial labor, I'm gonna need to cheer myself up."

And if he was lucky, he'd also come up with a plan to find another three thousand-odd terras to get his star-drive fixed.

On the streets of Boston Prime lurked no fewer than eight Mordecais. None of them would notice it, of course, but everyone who saw them perceived them as a tall, scrawny wizard with a baggy-sleeved shirt and a pack slung over one shoulder. Only someone as talented as Mordecai would be able to tell which was which without resorting to vulgar displays of revelatory magic. Every time he found himself at a crossroads or crowded terminal, he found a likely candidate heading in another direction and deputized them as a new doppelganger. Yet every time he sent another false Mordecai to muddle his path, he was still left with the pervasive feeling of being followed.

If he could not buy himself a moment's peace from whoever was pursuing him, his plan might fall dead at his feet. Mordecai tried something more creative. He stopped at a shuttle terminal—nothing fancy, just a simple intra-hemispheric depot. Giving a paranoid look over his shoulder, he ducked into the men's washroom. In the privacy of his stall, he paused to collect his thoughts, counting to one hundred with a slow, even cadence in his head. He emerged and washed his hands, studying a gentleman at the sink beside him —tall, wide shoulders, with a gray suit and matching hair, receding from the brow. The man carried a business attaché case.

When Mordecai left that washroom, he was the one with the grey suit and hair, his knapsack transformed to appear as an attaché case. The false Mordecai who followed him out sported a beard and glasses that Mordecai lacked, and wore different clothing, but in all other ways looked just like him, right down to the case that appeared as a knapsack, dangling casually from his hand.

Mordecai never discovered his pursuer. He stood by a departure and arrival board and watched as his body double boarded a flight to London Prime. By the time the shuttle to London lifted off, the sensation of a wizard concealed in close proximity vanished. It had to have been one of Wenling's lackeys, he had assumed initially. But the more he thought about it, he wondered if it had been Pao Wenling herself following him. It certainly would have explained his inability to pinpoint his pursuer. As he watched the shuttle disappear into the distance, he raised a finger to his temple in a quiet salute.

Free from his tail, Mordecai made for the theater district, resuming his own form. At the Orpheum, he slipped past two magic-befuddled doormen and made his way backstage. "Where can I find Chuck Ramsey?" Mordecai asked a flunky who stood with datapad in hand, updating the flatvid boards that showed what was playing at the theater.

"That lot's shipping offworld," the flunky replied. "Try Logan Starport. His ship is the *Radiocity.*" The lad pronounced it like some sort of chemical process, but being a wizard, Mordecai's mind parsed things differently. He instantly saw a likely spelling in his head, pulled it apart, and reattached it as Radio City, a New York Prime theater just as famous as the Orpheum. Ramsey had a consistent style; he'd give him that much.

Mordecai reached into a pocket and grabbed a ten-terra coin. He muttered a few words over it and tossed it to the flunky. "I was never here," he said, as the coin was in midair. By the time the lad caught hold of that coin, he had no inkling of having met Mordecai The Brown. For all that theater worker knew, he had found the coin along the back alleyway.

Logan Starport was the hub of Boston Prime, despite being located on the waterfront. Mordecai hopped into the first taxi he found and paid hardcoin to get there. He wasn't about to risk using his Convocation tab for anything... perhaps ever again. As the city blurred by, Mordecai fought the impulse to hide his hands in his sleeves. He went so far as to roll them up to the elbow to hide the wide, conspicuous openings.

At the starport, Mordecai was whisked into a world rife with science. Holovid advertisements, security-scan checkpoints, self-propelled luggage transports, and voice-interactive information kiosks. He held his breath as he passed by the worst of the scientific devices, keeping even his most casual uses of magic at bay lest he set one of them malfunctioning and draw attention to himself. Finding a lone starship in the jumble of humanity and blaring holovids was more daunting than he expected. For a moment, he considered striking up a conversation with one of the kiosks, but he had never spoken with a machine before. Would one even talk to a wizard? He hated them; would they hate him right back?

Security cameras throughout the starport would be recording him every step of his search, but one magic that he would not relinquish was the one that kept his features indistinct to science. No techno-gadget was going to do better than a finger-painted picture of Mordecai while he was in the starport. Humans were another matter. A lone traveler might not attract attention, but one who asked for directions might stick in someone's mind. Wiping memories was a simple enough task in an empty theater, but there were wards against those sorts of magic in high-security areas.

Mordecai's eyes widened. There was a group of laaku passing by, wearing uniforms for Phabian Starways, the major interstellar passenger service of their homeworld. The laaku were chimp-like, resembling those distant ancestors more closely than humans mirrored the great apes from which they diverged in pre-historic times. Shorter, quadridexterous, and covered in short fur, they were the only xeno-species allowed to freely roam Earth. Despite being humanity's closest ally and a founding member of the Allied Races of the Galactic Ocean, there was a common perception that all laaku looked alike. Among laaku, that perception was inverted, and they found all humans more or less identical. Mordecai could use that.

"Excuse me, sir?" Mordecai asked one of them. The laaku stopped and craned his neck up at a human twice his height. He wore a name badge that identified him as Korvin, with some laaku script beneath that likely said the same thing.

"Can I help you?" Korvin replied in English with just the

barest hint of a laaku accent. Master collaborators, the laaku had largely embraced Earth culture, and many spoke English better than their native tongue. It was a survival technique that had made them prosperous where other species saw their worlds bombarded from orbit and occupied.

Mordecai smiled. "This is my first time in a starport, and I'm lost. Can you show me where I can find the *Radio City*?"

Korvin exchanged an amused glance with one of his co-workers and took Mordecai to a holovid map, buzzing through a rapid-fire explanation that ended with a simple instruction on which way to go. Had Mordecai been able to grasp the process, he was sure Korvin had showed him enough to find any ship he ever needed to, but all that he had gotten from the exchange was a concourse number and landing pad. It was enough.

Logan Starport might have been a Byzantine labyrinth, but it had good, plain-painted signs. Permanent. Non-digital. Non-holo. Just words on flat panels, dangling over every intersection. Mordecai followed them to Concourse J, Pad 1172.

Given all the gadgetry scattered around the starport, he was sure he had been scanned a dozen or more times on his way, but nothing made a fuss. He came out into the open sky to find a starship that looked... well, very starship-like to Mordecai. It was dishwater gray and bigger than his house, though not by much. The side of the front bit was painted with the name "RADIOCITY" in bold letters, flaked away in spots but clearly legible.

Music came from the ramp around back, where men with hovering skids and robotic arms carted things aboard. Mort listened to Chuck Ramsey's voice singing along as he made his way around the ship—some sort of backhanded ode to Boston

Prime that he had never heard. The comedian was playing an acoustic guitar that sounded like it might have been half a note out of tune. When Mordecai rounded the corner, the song stopped.

"Well, how's about that?" Chuck said, standing and setting aside a guitar with a frayed strap and the cherry wood buffed smooth where the player's hands rubbed over the years. "Mort! Didn't expect to be seeing you... well, ever, frankly. We don't get back to Earth much, and what're the odds, you know?"

Mordecai stepped onto the ramp, glancing over his shoulder to see if any of the freight loaders might be listening. "Hey, Chuck. Any chance you might take on a passenger?"

Chuck pulled back and narrowed his eyes, but a smirk spread on his face at the same time. "Thought you were some fancy-pants real wizard, not some star-drive mechanic. Never heard of wizards traveling offworld much, except for navy attack dogs or terramancers."

"I have pressing business with the Convocation that involves being anywhere but here."

"I see," Chuck said. Their eyes met, and Mordecai had the impression that Chuck Ramsey was sizing him up, weighing him, and deciding whether there was room aboard his ship for both Mordecai and the trouble he was bringing with him.

"You told me you had troubles with your star-drive," Mordecai said.

"You gonna sign on as a mechanic?" Chuck asked, crossing his arms and cocking his head.

Mordecai harrumphed. "Please... with me aboard, you won't need a star-drive. All those gizmos do is imitate what a real wizard could manage. You not only won't have to pay for constant repairs and getting towed back to realspace, you'll be able to outrun... well anything without a wizard as good as I am."

Chuck gave him a shrewd look. Terras floated in his eyes, weighing against whatever trouble Mordecai might be running from. "Deal. Come on aboard. I gotta watch these lift-loaders, but Bradley can show you around." He stuck out a hand, and the two men shook.

Bradley Carlin Ramsey looked ecstatic to have a live wizard aboard. "You can bunk with me," he insisted. "You're old, so I'll take the top bunk so you don't have to climb so much. You know... I always wanted to be a pilot, but if you could teach me to be a wizard, that would be far out!" The boy had obviously been listening to too much of his father's old twentieth-century material and picked up the archaic lingo.

"Whatever you grow up to be, just don't become what everyone expects of you," Mordecai said, wagging a finger and trying to sound sage. "People like that are boring as shit."

Bradley looked around, ducked his head, and whispered. "Shit's a bad word."

"Kid, I'm an expert on bad words, and trust me, 'shit' doesn't make the top one hundred." Every word of the Tome of Bleeding Thoughts qualified, he thought bitterly, the book that had cost him his life on Earth.

Nancy lifted her chin as the top pearl button on her collar popped through its buttonhole. It took three tries and a firm admonition to her fingers to stop shaking. Her reflection in the dressing table mirror looked back with a firm set of jaw and steely blue eyes. The woman behind the glass had the poise of a sculpture, the bearing of a queen, and the presence of a mighty sorceress—so long as she kept her trembling hands out of view.

Annabeth approached, heels clacking as she topped the stairs at the end of the hall and headed for the royal suite. "Ma'am, the hover is here."

Nancy opened her mouth to speak. No sound came on the first try. She wetted her lips and made a second attempt. "I'll be down presently. Ceddie and Cassie are with the tutors?"

"Yes, ma'am."

"Very good. See to the breakfast plates and take the rest of the day off."

"Ma'am?"

"You heard me correctly."

The maid curtsied. "Of course, ma'am. Thank you, ma'am."

Nancy wondered when she'd become accustomed to such deference as a matter of course. *She* hadn't grown up a Brown. Now, with Mort running from the Grand Council's investigators, she wondered how long such treatment might persist.

Today's foray across the Atlantic would play heavily into an answer to that question.

She bustled down the stairs, fidgeting with the rings on her fingers and the gem set into her necklace. Heirlooms. If things went badly, they might not make the return trip with her that evening.

The pilot of the hover held the door for her and closed it behind her with the quiet efficiency of a butler. When he took his seat at the controls, all he said was, "Headington?"

"That's right," Nancy confirmed, keeping her hands stuffed inside opposing sleeves. And with that, the hover lifted off.

Boston's skyline whisked by in seconds. Then, they were over the ocean. Nancy shut her eyes and measured her breathing, rehearsing how she'd make her case.

The transatlantic flight was far too short for her to reach any satisfactory draft of the conversation. Before she knew it, the shining cities of the British Isles raced beneath the hover. Geography eluded her as the towering spires and glittering, multi-story complexes rolled across the countryside like terrain with no elemental earth visible to support them.

Soon enough, the illusion that Britain was composed of naught but glassteel and plastic gave way before a manicured and tended patch of greenery not so different from the wizardly conclave within Boston Prime.

Oxford University.

The sibling rivalry between Boston Prime's Harvard and the esteemed old university on the far side of the pond was of little concern to most with no affiliation to either. However, despite living in the Convocation's back garden and a decade since graduation, Oxford was a second home for Nancy.

Slowing to local ground traffic speeds, the hover swooped low and breezed across the campus, a paradise of old-world charm amid a world of modernity and excess. Nancy allowed herself a brief reminiscence before the reminder that meeting Mort here was the origin of her present troubles.

To the east of campus lay Headington, a bedroom community acting as a floodgate to the world of science and technology beyond. Among the esteemed residents was the head of the Intergalactic Union of Terramancers, Alastair The Brown.

Never mind that no sane wizard had so much as boasted of contact with a neighboring galaxy, let alone negotiated a membership agreement with one. The inclusion of such an aggrandizing boast in their name told outsiders all they needed to know about Earth's premier—and only official—organization of terramancers.

The hover departed, having deposited Nancy at the end of a long cobblestone path to the front door of 171 London Road. Keeping her hands tucked in her sleeves, Nancy reminded herself that one of the non-magical rings she wore was better protection than any ward or shield she might possess: her wedding ring.

Alastair was her father-in-law. She was mother to his only two grandchildren, though Mort's sister Sarajah was getting serious with Lord McGowan. Until that relationship bore fruit, she enjoyed a semi-irreplaceable spot in the family hierarchy.

When she reached the ornate iron front door, she didn't have to expose a hand to lift the knocker. The door opened, held by a bowing Clancy, Alastair's manservant.

"Good morning, madame. The master is expecting you."

"But I didn't send word ahead."

While Nancy hadn't gone to extraordinary lengths to conceal her plans, neither had she told anyone but the pilot where she was heading today. Accepting direction from Clancy's swept hand, she entered and felt the warmth of familiar surroundings. Despite Mort living in the dormitories, this had still been his family home while they were dating.

"About time you showed up," Alastair groused from the second-floor landing, drawing Nancy's gaze upward. The uncanny resemblance to both Nebuchadnezzar and Mordecai never failed to strike her after not seeing one of them for a while. She wondered how long it might be before little Cedric began to bear the same similarity in appearance.

"How did you know I'd come?" Nancy asked. She couldn't

deny he'd been anticipating her arrival, but not knowing how nagged at her. Her near future might involve a great deal of subterfuge. Any insight might help her along the way.

"Tea. Earl Grey. For two," he snapped at Clancy, who accepted his employer's ire with studious indifference. Then, as if the interlude hadn't taken place, he returned his attention to his daughter-in-law. "How could you not? Mordecai's gone and done it. Everyone knows it. But they'll pussyfoot around the issue until his deadline is up. You've got until then to decide whether to cooperate with Wenling's inquisition or hide behind that gold ring on your finger."

Self-consciously, Nancy twisted the wedding band on her left ring finger. Even hidden by her sleeves, she knew Alastair would notice. "What do I do? I'm not a politician."

Alastair snorted. The noise must have been hereditary, since both Mort and the late Nebuchadnezzar sounded just like him. "Neither is he. He should have stuck to Acquisitions and stayed off the Grand Council."

Clancy returned with a tea setting in far less time than a non-wizard ought to have been able to brew a proper kettle. Nancy knew better than to object. After all, Alastair had known she was coming. The two of them took chairs in the sitting room, where the scent of burning cedar wafted from a hearth fire. Rolling her sleeves to mid-forearm, Nancy accepted her accustomed milk and two sugars from Clancy and tried to keep her hand steady as she whirled the silver teaspoon to mix the additives.

Alastair seemed piqued but otherwise utterly at ease. "So, which way are you leaning?"

"I want to help him!" Nancy blurted. She brought up her other hand to steady the cup she was raising to her lips. Squeezing her eyes shut, she seethed a breath and took a sip.

"No one would think less of you if you didn't."

Nancy choked. "What? Of course, they would! I'm his wife. I'm the head of the Widows Outreach Fund. I'm—"

"You'll have to resign from that."

Pausing mid-rant, just as the momentum was building and putting her feet beneath her, Nancy halted. "Whatever for?"

"Wizard killed in the line of duty..."

Nancy nodded along. He wasn't telling her anything that wasn't written into the fund's charter.

"Wives, husbands, children left without support."

Setting down her teacup, Nancy spread her hands. "Yes? Your point?"

"Don't you see how that might be seen as gauche when it's Mordecai sending you clients?"

Drawing up indignantly in her seat, Nancy snapped back, "They're not 'clients.' They're victims. And they need emotional support as much as financial, if not more."

"And how would *you* feel receiving pity alms from Mordecai's murderer? Would you want to eat scones and cry on the shoulder of his killer's husband?"

"You're... you're presupposing..." Nancy gulped.

Alastair's close-lipped smile told her she was finally starting to understand.

"But he's one of the good guys," Nancy protested. "He hunts down dark wizards. He's not one of them."

"Bullshit, he's not!" Alastair shouted, startling Nancy into dropping her tea just as she picked the cup up again. The priceless porcelain would have shattered on the marble floor if Alastair hadn't caught it with telekinesis and guided both the cup and spilled liquid back to her hand. "That position isn't for the faint of heart. It's not for the squeamish. My father used to tell me stories of that job that gave me nightmares for most of my youth."

With a voice tiny as a mouse, Nancy dared ask, "Is that why you didn't come to the house?"

"I wouldn't have been popular celebrating while my brothers and cousins pretended to cry."

"No one's going to be celebrating or crying over Mort. He might have decided to run, but he won't be killing anyone unless he runs into actual dark wizards." Putting a hand to her forehead, she couldn't believe she needed to say that out loud. "I don't know what could have come over him in the first place."

"According to my sources, he entered the Plundered Tomes shortly after talking with my father. I'd bet the estate that old relic put him up to it."

Nancy shook her head. "I knew you two never got along, but..."

"I can say this because they're both gone now. Because it's *safe* now. Nebuchadnezzar The Brown was one of the few wizards I've ever truly feared. And Mordecai, despite all my efforts, insisted on following his footsteps. There *will* be deaths. If he'd stayed, a good lawyer might have gotten him off on a dying-request exemption. But he's running, and he's dangerous, and there will be blood and ash in his wake when they send the kill squads after him."

"Kill... squads...?" Nancy had heard about the justice the Convocation dished out, on occasion, to less creative villains among wizardkind. Invent a novel spell to turn bears into vampires, and they'd send librarians to claim the research and dispose of the one responsible. For more mundane capital offenses, Wenling's department had teams practiced in the arts of overwhelming lone wizards, no matter how powerful.

For the life of her, she couldn't picture Mort as a common criminal.

With a huff, Alastair threw himself back in his chair. "I wouldn't worry about my son. Resign your position. 2540 will be a year of consoling the widows and orphans."

"Mort said he'd look for a replacement copy of the—"

"Bah!" Alastair waved her off. Then he narrowed one eye and wagged a finger. "Mark my words. That one... he's going to relish the duels to come. There's a reason *he* goes off without backup to execute aberrant researchers. No one listened to me. They told me to stick to terramancy. Let the boy follow his talents. Well, who's paranoid now? Nancy, I've never liked you. Mordecai should have waited until he was in his fifties to marry. But for better or worse, you're the mother of my first two grandchildren."

It hurt hearing it so bluntly, but Alastair's disapproval of Mort had long leaked over to her. But the idea of marrying an older wizard was all wrapped up in nonsense about waiting for a man to "come into his power." Whom could she have loved who held a candle before the raging inferno of Mordecai The Brown?

Not that anyone was going to take *her* side in this family.

"I'd rather they grow up with their father around."

Leaning forward and resting an elbow on his knee, Alastair looked her straight in the eye. Nancy held her ground and didn't look away. "This is the best advice I'll ever give, so listen carefully. Children are better off without certain kinds of father."

The boarding ramp closed.

The waiting began.

From the ship's living room, Mordecai listened in as Chuck argued with orbital traffic control. Without straining his ears or enacting magic, Mort couldn't make out the other half of the conversation. The comedian, however, had a voice that could batter down brickwork.

"Yeah. I know that ... No, I'm looking for an outbound vector toward Io ... Uh huh ... Right ... I know that's what I filed when I landed. I changed my mind ... I realize the visitor's center is closed. I just promised my kids a flyby. I really don't know what business it is of yours. I'm *leaving* Earth, not arriving ... Oh, well sure. Why didn't you just say so?"

Mordecai strained his imagination to fill in the missing jigsaw bits of the conversation. Not being a fool, he laid the irregular chunks of cardboard out in his head and painted in the details. Chuck had to have been making a change to a flight plan he'd previously filed with the datapad-pushers floating around in space stations above Earth's sky. Curiously, the fellow seemed to realize that manual astral drops from Earth orbit might be seen as suspicious and was booking them travel through one of the low-unit astral gates that operated entirely within the Sol system.

Instead, they were hopping out to the Jovian moon of Io. Father had taken Mordecai there as a boy, back before he'd given up on making a terramancer of him. The Moon of Ice and Fire, they called it. Cold enough to freeze polar bears solid with enough volcanoes to put on proper fireworks shows often enough to sell tickets.

"Is this your first time on a ship?" Bradley asked.

Mordecai grunted. "Hardly."

"The smallest?"

With a pause to measure his brief inspection of the vessel

against his recollection of the Convocation's nameless shuttle. "Close, but also no."

Up front, Chuck had made an apparent breakthrough while his eldest son was yammering. He strode into the room grinning like a politician. "Great news. Autopilot's set. We'll be at Io in a couple hours. From there, I expect you can take over."

"Io, huh?" Mordecai asked. "A little last-minute sightseeing before putting Sol behind us?"

"We saved enough on the star-drive repairs that I could pay the gate fee. Figured I'd let you get settled in before you have to conjure the demons of the nether universe."

Mordecai was half tempted to tell Chuck just how little the magic would tax him, but better to make the guy think his new wizard was indispensable. Of course, there were few wizards less dispensable than Mordecai The Brown, but jamming that notion into what by quick reckoning was going to prove to be an unreasonably thick skull, he didn't want to leave any room for doubt.

A scent of chocolate wandered in from the kitchen. Becky called out, "Who wants brownies?"

"Me!" Bradley shot up his hand.

The two little ones, Mike and Rhiannon he recalled, raced in from their bedroom, shrieking in joy. The boy looked to be about Cedric's age, though feral in the way that scientifically raised children generally were. The girl was perhaps two years younger, still in diapers.

Becky came in with a platter in hand, piled with perfectly formed squares of dense, cakey chocolate. "We've got chocolate and garbage-puke flavored."

Mordecai raised an eyebrow.

Chuck shot him a wink as he plucked one of a pair of

brownies set aside at the edge of the plate. The larger pile angled in front of the children's greedy hands. The comedian took a bite, and with his mouth full, advised Mordecai, "I'd stick to the chocolate. Garbage-puke is an acquired taste, and you've got some work coming up."

Aha. So, this was code for the sake of the kids. While he never partook himself, plenty of lesser wizards availed themselves of mild hallucinogens to expand their imaginative powers. Struggle enough in practical magics, and some exasperated tutor would eventually hand a student a pipe and something to smoke with it. The bluebloods and prodigies often joked that the nose-wrinkling stench was the sign of a mind gone rotten.

Mordecai partook out of politeness and managed to keep to himself that it tasted like it had been warmed between the cheeks of some robot's buttocks. He'd eaten light that day, and anything felt good entering the stomach, even a lump of chemicals impersonating baked goods.

The little ones played on the floor with blocks and plastic figurines after their snack. Bradley took it upon himself to act as a tour guide in a room with precisely zero interesting features. Amazingly, the boy managed to keep up a nearly nonstop stream-of-thought history of the vessel, its occupants, and the milquetoast adventures they'd had in his brief lifetime.

It was almost enough to distract Mordecai from the persistent worry about how long it might be before the pursuit began in earnest. It wouldn't be the Convocation's first instinct to look offworld. He'd never made a secret of his disdain for the uncivilized planets of the galaxy—and unlike many, he lumped Orion and even Mars right in with the border colonies in that regard.

But Wenling was no fool. She'd figure out he'd jumped

planet. Then the race was truly on... one that might last the rest of Mordecai's life, however long that might be.

Becky bustled about the ship, half keeping the larval scientists from harming themselves and half fussing pointlessly over minutiae. She hummed unfamiliar tunes as she worked. When she wandered to a blank spot on the wall and touched a panel, Mort at first thought little enough of it.

Mort felt the tingle.

They'd just passed through another astral gate and back to realspace. The window control Becky had activated brought down a protective screen, revealing a bank of windows looking out at the familiar, miserable little moon Io.

Chuck came back from the cockpit, clapping his hands together sharply and rubbing them as if he expected to start a fire. "Here we are. I pulled us out of traffic. How long until we can flow on out of this reality?"

Given the snacks on this ship, Mordecai wasn't certain whether Chuck was referring to the same reality the wizards and children aboard were occupying, but he left that discussion for another time. He cleared his throat. "Time to earn my keep."

He retrieved his pack from the floor and dug around inside. When his hand closed around a familiar wooden surface, he pulled. An Earthwood staff as tall as he was slid out and took on its full length.

Bradley gawked open-mouthed. "How'd you do that?"

Mordecai scowled. "Do what?"

The boy pointed. "It's bigger than your backpack. How'd it fit in there?"

What a poor, deprived life these technology-addled children lived, where common magic beheld such wonders.

"It's like a magic trick," Chuck answered for him. "Smoke and mirrors."

"Except without any smoke or mirrors," Mordecai clarified. He rubbed his chin. "When you have too many clothes to fit in a suitcase, what do you do?"

The boy brightened. "I sit on it while Mom zips!"

"Same theory. Laundry is infinitely compressible."

"But you can't squish a stick that big," Bradley protested.

"*You* can't. I most certainly can. Now, if you all don't mind. I could use a quiet moment here."

A hush fell over the ship. Even the toddler seemed intent on watching to see what miracle was coming.

Since he was a guest on this ship, Mordecai decided to put on a show. Chuck was a showman, after all. Closing his eyes, Mort took the staff in both hands and chanted in Aramaic. It was the default language generally agreed upon to sound the most mystical to the uninitiated.

Using a vocabulary spoken only among a minority of well-educated wizards, he addressed the universe itself. *Nice smooth ride. Comfortably deep. No particular rush.*

A sensation akin to a trip down a playground slide, the *Radio City* and all aboard whooshed away from the three spatial dimensions of the Milky Way in a direction that was simultaneously perpendicular to all of them.

When he opened his eyes, it was dark in the ship. The omnipresent hum of engines and environmental technologies shouted its absence.

Through the open windows, the pale gray of astral space yawned, blank and infinite. There was just enough of an ambient glow to it that faint silhouettes inhabited the ship.

Chuck cleared his throat. "You know, my fault for not

mentioning this, but... we kinda need the *rest* of the ship to keep working for this plan to come out ahead."

Mordecai harrumphed. "Oh ye of little faith. Give it a minute. The doodads are ornery. They'll get over it."

True to his word, the science wobbled back to its old familiar static self, and the technological devices reliant upon it spluttered back to work soon after.

An hour later, Mordecai sat on the couch beside Bradley as the latter yammered about the holovid program they were watching. Mordecai divided his attention between formulating appropriate verbal replies and wondering where his life had gone so horribly wrong.

His one grand gesture completed, he was reduced to a mere starliner passenger. Destination: mediocrity.

▭

"Three days come, and three days gone," Bertram Hancock intoned formally, voice rising to the vaulted ceiling of the council chamber as if he were a one-man choir. The Grand Council had reconvened on a crisp autumn Monday after a weekend of reprieve for the wayward librarian who'd so plainly failed in his duties. "Where is Mordecai The Brown?"

Two seats at the meeting table remained empty. One, by tradition, was reserved for guests of the Grand Council. The other belonged to the absent member of the assemblage. Though oftentimes other commitments kept the chair holders away, and often the council met with barely a quorum, none had dared miss this one.

None but the one whose absence was damning.

Pao Wenling rose from her place in the Third Seat. "At present, the whereabouts of Mordecai The Brown are unknown."

Silence met her declaration.

Walls of thick stone blocked the din and clamor of the college campus upon whose grounds the Grand Council met. In the test of wills between the First and Third Seats, nervous swallows and the brushing of fabric against fabric as councilors shifted in their chairs could be heard clearly around the chamber.

"How?" Bertram asked at length.

"He enjoys matching wits with dark wizards for a lark," Wenling replied with acid on her tongue. "I assigned twelve inquisitors to the search. I even pulled in a team from Luna to assist. He first spotted his surveillance team at the Orpheum Theater. After that, we redoubled our efforts to maintain secrecy in the hopes he might lead us to where he'd hidden the stolen tome. Despite our best efforts, he slipped away from our monitoring teams. It is quite probable that he is no longer in Boston Prime."

Bertram glowered past the Second Chair, Lissa Marrowstack, who tried to slouch away from scrutiny, and fixed the weight of his disapproval on the chief inquisitor. "Where is he *now*?"

"We've expanded the search. Field offices across North America and Europe have joined our efforts. We're canvassing all locations the fugitive has ties to and interviewing known associates."

"That doesn't answer my—"

"Lay off, Bert," Ronald Sternenlicht cut in from the Fourth Chair. "This isn't a campaign speech. Wenling knows her business. Let's circle this back to the book that's missing. What have you learned about it?"

Wenling lifted a stack of old parchment and drew a pair of spectacles through which to view them. "The only record of the contents of the *Tome of Bleeding Thoughts* was recorded by Nebuchadnezzar The Brown in 2501. I won't read the entirety here, but the relevant passage is as follows...

'It is my professional conclusion that whatever theories on mind and thought it sought to explore, the book itself left a legacy as primarily an agent of destruction of the mind that reads it. It is unfailingly lethal to the unwary mind, and it is only thanks to extremes of both caution and willpower that I was able to glean the contents concealed between its covers. My recommendation is that this volume be confined for eternity to the most secure vault in the Plundered Tomes.'"

Calm, measured footsteps approached from the shadows of the room in the direction of the guest entrance. "Those were the days," called out Avril Cruz, the lone non-wizard on the day's agenda. "I can only imagine if we were still allowed to ship prisoners off to be interrogated or mysteriously disappeared."

"Welcome, Deputy Director," Bertram replied on behalf of the council. "If you'd take a seat, we'll be with you shortly."

"In summary," Wenling continued, "the only one with a knowledge of that book's contents recently passed away, and the only one present at the moment of death was Mordecai The Brown."

"We have to assume he's read it and survived," Bertram stated. "Get someone to pore over Nebuchadnezzar's research for additional insights. But for the time being, we have to assume that Mordecai The Brown isn't acting rationally and may be in the thrall of a Plundered Tome."

"Is this something that happens often?" Deputy Director Cruz asked. "Books taking control of wizards?"

Bertram scowled. "You're out of order."

Flinging her notes on the *Tome of Bleeding Thoughts* to the table, Wenling snapped, "Recognize her and let's get on with this. Maybe an outside perspective will help us chart these unfamiliar stars."

"Fine. Deputy Director, please state your full name and position," Bertram instructed curtly.

"My name is Avril Luisa Cruz, I have worked for Earth Interstellar Enhanced Investigative Organization for thirty-seven years and have served as Deputy Director for the past five. Director Yang was on Mars when news of the crisis broke, or he'd have come himself."

"Deputy Director, have you notified your agency that this fugitive is to be considered armed and lethal?" Bertram asked.

Cruz didn't flinch. "It's Earth Interstellar standard operating procedure to defer to Convocation justice whenever practicable."

"Not practicable," Wenling said. "Under no circumstance should non-wizards approach Mordecai The Brown or attempt to apprehend him. If he is spotted, simply convey his location to us."

Cruz set her jaw. "With all due respect, I must object. It's one thing calling a local outreach center to have the Convocation round up drunk and disorderly wizards. But from what I'm hearing, this wizard may be a hazard to civilians. Earth Interstellar *does* have certain countermeasures that have proved useful in dealing with wizards in the—"

Before she could say "past," Wenling cut her off. "*With all due respect,*" she echoed darkly, "you have never faced a threat like this one. When wizards go bad, we have teams we send to eliminate the threat."

"I've always admired—and envied a little—how clean you keep your house."

"There is a hierarchy to these teams. Most of your comms to us are to deal with commonplace nuisances. However, there are elite teams dedicated to hunting down and neutralizing more potent threats. Minds like iron. Decades of experience. The very best got to work in the Library of the Plundered Tomes, tracing the work of madmen to the source and combating magical powers of unknown breadth and provenance."

"And that's who you've lost," Cruz commented as she nodded along.

"No," Wenling said coldly. "We lost the Guardian of the Plundered Tomes. He's the last line of defense when one of our elite assassins goes rogue. He's the one responsible for protecting us from the worst monsters the Convocation has ever faced. Single-handedly. Per ancient laws that predate transatlantic sailing, it is the only position within the Convocation wherein the holder can be challenged to a duel to the death by a prospective replacement.

"So, Deputy Director, if anyone in your organization or local law enforcement encounter Mordecai The Brown, report his location and nothing more."

Deputy Director Cruz nodded. "Understood."

Shoulders sagging, Bertram added, "And please keep this quiet. The last thing the Convocation needs is a scandal in front of the technologists."

Mordecai stood watch from the top of the *Radio City's* cargo ramp as a ground crew unloaded crates. The space was little more than a storage shed accessible from both inside and outside the ship. They'd arrived on Orion IV half an hour ago, bathed beneath the otherworldliness of a blue sun. Most Earthlings considered the colonies to all be varying degrees of uncivilized, though Mars and Orion IV were close enough that few quibbled over the difference, alongside the laaku homeworld of Phabian.

To Mort, it was a technocracy without end. At least Earth had enclaves of timeless civility in the various nature preserves and Convocation strongholds.

"I bet you've never been offworld before," Bradley commented brightly. "Dad says wizards don't like to travel."

"Been lots of places. Probably more than you." Despite his spacer lifestyle, the boy was younger than Mordecai's socks.

"Oh yeah?" the boy replied, clearly taking his claim as a challenge. "I've been to Mars, Ganymede, Kepler, New Venice, Hadriss, twice to Phabian ..."

"Fine," Mordecai allowed, not wishing to make an argument of it. He could see that pressing his claim here might involve either a thorough accounting of his occupational travels or a degree of lying that he simply wasn't in the mood for. "Maybe you've been to more than I've given you credit for."

"It's on account of Dad's routine getting old fast. And if you think locals get bored of him, just wait until he starts trying out new material on you."

Mordecai raised an eyebrow. "What makes you think I'm sticking around? Once these load-luggers toddle off, I'll see about realigning your star-drive."

The boy's face fell. "But..."

"Look. It was a lucky coincidence that you and your family were leaving Earth about the time I needed a ride. That's all. I'll tell your parents when they're done haggling."

Chuck and Becky stood apart from the loading crew, in the shade of the warehouse. By the hand gestures from Chuck, he was losing an argument. Why did they have to bicker in front of Rhiannon, held on her mother's hip? It was unseemly, undercutting parental authority. Mordecai and Nancy disagreed often enough but had the sense to hide it from the children.

When a pang of guilt rose inside him, a defense mechanism kicked in and devised a distraction. "Where's your brother?" The middle Ramsey child was missing in action.

"He's watching Strawberry Space Heroes in the living room. He won't budge until it's over."

Mordecai harrumphed. What would be the cost of pacifying the minds of these children with holovids? Then again, presumably the same parenting had produced Bradley, who seemed sharp enough of wit for a technologist lad.

Chuck stomped over, combing a hand through his hair. Becky took Rhiannon and headed for a coffee and pastry shop across the street called Cream, Sugar, and Frosting. The comedian had clearly come off the worse for the argument with his spouse. "Brad, go make yourself a sandwich."

The boy pointed. "But Mom—"

"She's getting coffees. You can comm her and have her grab you one, too. No desserts."

"OK..." Bradley replied, hanging his head.

Once the boy was gone inside the ship, Chuck held up a finger and crept to the door. Balling a fist, he slammed it against the steel surface. A startled yelp sounded from the far side. "Sorry. He does that. Now... I had a word with the ball and chain."

They paused while the guys with the grav sleds came back for another stack of crates.

"I noticed," Mordecai replied once they were alone again.

"You got a place to stay planetside?"

Mordecai shook his head. "No need to worry about me. I'll jigger up something to get your star-drive working and be on my way."

"It's nothing personal," Chuck continued. "It's just... that whole astral business spooked Becky pretty good. Kids. Life support failures. She's a little particular."

The outage had lasted all of two minutes. They hadn't been in any danger. But from a scientific viewpoint, Mordecai could imagine how a parent might worry for the safety of young children—worrying was half of what parenting was all about.

Mordecai stuck out a hand, and Chuck shook it. "No hard feelings. Not for nothing, but you rune up a few obsidian rods, and you can get away with hardly a flicker of the lights."

It took him all of ten minutes to cleanse the aura fouling the star-drive and orient the crystals to proper astral orientation. With the abuse the device obviously had seen, he gave it another few weeks before the gadget broke down again. As a parting gift, he tweaked the ship's gravity stone, correcting an anomalous two percent added weight over and above Earth Standard; while the discrepancy had been within terramancers' standards for colonial habitation, he'd been noticing it all trip.

Five minutes after that, Mordecai collected his few belongings and said his goodbyes. He waved to Becky and Rhiannon as they exited the coffee shop on his way past.

Then, free from Convocation surveillance, Mordecai The Brown disappeared into the vast cityscape of Orion IV.

The stone floor echoed beneath Nancy's high-heeled boots. She wore her Convocation medallion openly. Her lawyer had advised that she visibly remind the Grand Council that she was on their side. However, today's meeting wasn't with the full council. A set of winding stairs led beneath two stories underground, to a wine cellar of a conference room.

As she approached the open door, a voice called from inside. "Enter."

Rasputin Leonard, junior partner at Wexcombe, Dulcimer, and Leonard, gave a curt nod of assurance. He'd be present during the entire interrogation. She wouldn't have to worry about legalistic traps or self-incrimination with his aid.

Nancy stepped inside to find a modest wooden table with three chairs. The two to her left were empty. On the opposing side of the table sat Pao Wenling.

The chief inquisitor numbered among the few women who made Nancy Brown nervous. The two had only ever met at large, formal gatherings of the Convocation elite, at the sort of holiday and diplomatic dinner party to which Mort had to be dragged. While her husband, an old prune of a shriveled-up wizard, was a charming gentleman and a captivating storyteller, Wenling had a gaze that stripped the soul from the body.

"Inquisitor," Rasputin greeted her with a nod. He held the chair for Nancy before taking his seat.

"Thank you for coming this morning," Wenling said, making it sound as if the Convocation's invitation had been optional. She wore the same outfit to this deposition as she had for the Christmas Ball and the Hallow's Eve Masquerade. Rumor had it that she wrote poetry and was a painter of impressionistic leaning. Nancy had never seen behind the porcelain facade of the inquisitor.

Rasputin spared no time on preliminaries. "I'd like to remind you that my client is here voluntarily, and that she has not waived her marital rights against spousal incrimination."

"I am aware," Wenling replied.

Her voice sent a shiver up Nancy's spine. When Mort came home, there would be hell to pay for all she was going through over this. But before that, she had to do everything in her power to make sure his homecoming wasn't merely to stand trial and be executed.

"I trust you are aware of the reason for your presence here," the inquisitor continued.

"I've heard the rumors."

"They are more than rumors," Wenling assured her. "Mordecai The Brown has been charged with the theft of a vault-rated book from the Plundered Tomes. He has also abandoned his duties, missed a compulsory appearance before the Grand Council, and is suspected of reading the volume in question."

Nancy swallowed. The bleak stonework of the walls and the torch sconces providing the only illumination gave the interview room the feel of a dungeon cell. Intimidation tactics, she realized, but that didn't stop them from working.

"Ask your questions."

A book.

This was all over some stupid book. What could have possessed Mort to read one of those vile volumes anyway? Titillation? Pride? Was he looking for some secret lost to polite society? He would be answering so many more questions when she got ahold of him.

Wenling pressed her fingertips together. "When did you last see your husband?" Her eyes didn't blink as they bored into Nancy.

She couldn't detect any magic worming its way into her, trying to determine truth from lie. Such spells were illegal and inadmissible in court. But Nancy was on the far side of the Convocation justice system at the moment. If these people wanted answers, they'd worry about trials and sentences later.

Prompted by her sidelong glance, Rasputin gave a subtle nod. Part of his job was ensuring that even if Nancy missed the signs, Wenling wouldn't be able to enspell her. There was a general rule among wizardkind: Two wills are stronger than one. Wenling might have twisted their heads clean off their necks individually, but the pair of them could hold her in check.

Theoretically.

Mort was a notable exception to that rule. He went off into the unknown alone and hammered his will into the cracks of the universe. Odds didn't matter. Mordecai The Brown was a titan among lesser gods. Whether Wenling ought to be accorded that same degree of respect and fear was a matter Nancy hoped to avoid learning today.

"He left in the night. He said his goodbyes to the children in the small hours of Saturday."

"And you didn't inform the Convocation immediately?"

"My client doesn't have to answer that," Rasputin cut in briskly.

Nancy waved him off. "That's all right. No. I didn't. Both Mordecai and I were aware that the Convocation had him under surveillance. You knew he was going to be a flight risk before he did."

Cocking her head ever so slightly to the side, Wenling asked, "Did he give any indication where he might flee?"

"No. In fact he told me he wouldn't place me in a compromising position by telling me."

Wenling spread her hands. "And yet... here you are. Perhaps, even if his intention was to protect you, he has erred."

"I won't help you find him."

"You may refuse to answer my questions," Wenling conceded. "However, lying to an inquisitor is a crime even for a spouse."

Rasputin pushed back his chair with a noisy scrape. "Then I think we're done here. Nancy, let's—"

"SIT!" Wenling snapped.

Rasputin hastily returned to his seat.

"You have the right to refuse, but I have the authority to require you to sit here and individually refuse each question, on the record, if you choose not to cooperate."

"I don't see how that benefits either of us," Nancy replied stiffly. Could Wenling have some trick or trap planned for them? Her statement left the dangling bait for the chief inquisitor to expose her motives.

"Perhaps, if you hear what we are trying to accomplish, you might see how it is the best thing for Mordecai. We wish to return him home safely. No loss of life, either his or the hunters' sent to retrieve him."

Nancy's mouth went dry. "Hunters?"

It was a pleasant little euphemism for the Convocation's assassin squad. Nancy was under no illusions that Mort killed renegade wizards for a living, but hearing the script reversed to put her husband's name on the target list chilled her to the bone.

Wenling nodded. "Your husband has been behaving strangely. This episode is out of character. His grandfather and mentor dies. A Plundered Tome goes missing. Our understanding of the situation is incomplete, not the least of which because the only accounting of the contents of that Plundered Tome was written by the very same Nebuchadnezzar whose death appears to have catalyzed this chain of events. We are operating on what we consider both the most likely *and* worst-case scenario."

Nancy could barely manage a whisper. "What's that?"

"That Mordecai The Brown is under the thrall of a book known as the *Tome of Bleeding Thoughts*."

The idea that Mort wasn't himself lodged itself in Nancy's mind like a bur on a wool sweater.

It fit.

The timing.

The mania.

His last, clandestine meeting with his grandfather.

Had Nebuchadnezzar put Mort up to reading that book as part of one of his crazy immortality schemes?

Had it worked?

Who exactly was it walking around in Mort's body right now?

Before she could think better of it, she began to recount everything she knew of what Mort had done since his grandfather's passing and immediately before. Rasputin attempted to stop her, advising silence, but she ordered him to allow her testimony.

Wenling took notes with a quill, frantically scribbling Nancy's every word onto parchment.

"Now, as for speculation," Wenling said. "Where do you think Mordecai might seek to lie low? Who might shelter him? Would he turn to Alastair for protection? Is there anyone from his staff or old friends from Oxford he might enlist?"

Nancy weathered the barrage, mind reeling. None of that sounded like Mort. "I can't say what he might do if he's not himself. But the Mort I knew would sooner stand alone than turn to his father for help. He doesn't have any friends. I don't think his staff liked him, and it was mutual. Whatever you know about hunting wizards, he knows better. Wherever you think to look for him, he's thought of it and ruled it out. Whatever bait you put in your trap, he'll resist taking. You could endanger me or the children, and he'd steel himself to testing your willpower."

It hurt to admit that, but it also seemed like the best hedge against them actually trying.

"So, you think our search is doomed to failure," Wenling observed with a touch of sarcasm.

"No. But you need to think ahead of someone who knows all your standard methods."

Wenling scoffed. "So, as his wife, how would *you* recommend we find him? Bear in mind that if your aid brings about his capture, we will put all our resources to purging the malevolent influence from him. Where would *you* look?"

Nancy pursed her lips. A list of places Mort loved wafted through her memories. Vacations. Symposia. Historical sites. Then, as all the locales of Earth suggested reasons why each would fail Mort, the answer struck her. For a homebody of a wizard whose least favorite part of his job was the travel, it nonetheless made perfect sense.

"Anywhere but Earth."

Orion IV stretched on forever in all directions. Cities merged on into the next without clear delineation. Most of Mordecai's adventures off Earth had been to the kind of hellish backwaters that drew fugitives and secretive researchers, the kind of places where missing persons drew a shrug and mystical abominations could be written off as newly discovered local wildlife. It wasn't often that he found himself adrift among a populace nearly as dense and metropolitan as the grandiose old dames that orbited Sol.

For all its innumerable humans and occasional xenos, Mordecai had yet to spot a place he'd consider eating. How did so many sentient creatures crowd together without a respectable restaurant or so much as a roving hotdog vendor?

One garish canteen boasted nutrient goo shaped by laaku science into any food you fancied. Meats made from vegetables. Ice cream derived from meat. None of it sounded safe to consume.

Had he been in a touristy mood, he might have inquired as to what precisely "smucky" was. By the usage on signage at no fewer than three eateries, it had to be a local dish, possibly something known by an actual proper name back on Earth. But as he didn't relish the idea of calling attention to being from Sol, he avoided the issue entirely.

Bistros, cafes, greasy spoons, and bar and grills each presented him a reason to reject it: too snooty a clientele, foul odors wafting from the doors, a misspelling on the advertisements that spoke to a lack of attention to important details.

As the hours stretched on, Mordecai decided to find accommodations for the night. The blue sun was waning in the sky. He hadn't eaten since departing the *Radio City*—a peanut butter sandwich which he'd have traded all the slop houses of Orion IV to revisit—but any decent hotel ought to have room service.

Footsore and irritable, Mordecai marched himself into the Karling Arms Hotel and up to the front desk. Slinging his pack onto the counter, he gave his shoulder a rest and waited for someone to come offer the services common to a public house.

Minutes stretched on with no hint that he was going to be helped.

Guests filed in and out. A bellhop in a carnival-worthy uniform and hat lugged luggage on a grav-cart.

"Ahem..." Mordecai hinted as the lad trudged past him.

"Sir?"

"I've been waiting here twenty minutes," Mordecai guessed, not having checked for a clock or sundial upon his arrival.

"Is there a... problem with the terminal?" the bellhop asked carefully.

Mordecai followed the lad's gaze until discovering that the panel set at an angle into the front of the counter bore a coat of arms on a square background that perhaps glowed slightly. Reaching out a tentative finger, he tapped the screen.

The black eagle on a yellow shield vanished, replaced by text that read:

HOW MAY WE HELP YOU TODAY?

Below, tiny signs comprised a multiple-choice test of "check in," "check out," "amenities," "reservations," "guest services," and "feedback."

He must have scowled too long at the options, wondering how best to formulate his reply that he simply wanted a room for the night.

Now that he considered matters, his stay might last longer than one sleep and a hot shower. After all, he'd escaped his immediate pursuit on Earth. It might be months before Wenling and her band of merry morons exhausted their Earthbound options and considered the preposterous notion of a Brown roughing it offworld.

"Do you need help?" the bellhop asked.

That was a loaded question, one whose depths Mordecai The Brown was loath to plumb with a collegiate refugee hawking his labors at servants' wages. "I just want to rent a room."

Taking a hand from his grav-cart, the bellhop reached past and tapped "check in" on Mordecai's behalf.

"How many in your party?" the bellhop asked.

Raising an eyebrow, Mordecai quickly rejected the notion that the lad was propositioning him and replied, "Just me."

A flash of button taps and screens passed too quickly to register. "How many nights?"

"I haven't decided yet."

"I'll put you down for one night. You can always extend your stay if you choose."

"Then why ask?"

The bellhop maintained his pleasant attitude. "Some guests like to take care of all their logistics all at once. Now, if you just scan your thumb on the reader, you'll be charged a deposit of 325T for the night."

Mild curiosity nearly convinced him to press his thumb to the fingerprint-shaped pad the bellhop indicated. However, aside from the omnipresent worry of destroying a potentially fragile technological device, he knew that no good would come of such an intrusion.

"I don't have any digital money."

The bellhop straightened and cleared his throat. "I'm not actually authorized to handle hardcoin payments. But if you'll wait here, I've got to deliver luggage for one of our other guests, and I'll find you a manager who can."

"Much obliged," Mordecai replied with a businesslike nod.

As soon as the bellhop loaded his cargo onto one of the lobby's numerous lifts, he turned and fled as fast as decorum allowed.

Drat these scientists!

Digital money was a blight. Hardcoin was the currency of peasants and gangsters. One could hardly conduct commerce on Earth in hard currency without a scandal. Handling coinage was so... Martian.

It would have been the simplest of matters to wait for Pushy Carts-alot to return with his boss's boss and flash the Convocation sigil. A simple illusion in the palm of his hand would be all it would take to access unlimited credit for food, lodging, and basic necessities. The hotel would file a reimbursement form, ship it off to Diane's people in the Convocation Bursar's Office. A few months later, money would show up. Mordecai wasn't sure of the clockwork involved in between, but he'd heard enough complaints along his travels that he understood that it was neither prompt, nor efficient, and rife with corruption.

With Mordecai's luck, this once, they'd have their act together and flag a suspicious hotel for Wenling's watch-hawks to investigate.

The azure sunset glinted from steel-clad towers as Mordecai returned to the streets of some unknown city or district within the Orion IV ecumenopolis.

Nice as this planet was purported to be, only two worlds in all of ARGO space even boasted of being crime-free: Earth and Phabian. All the rest had an underworld of varying size and influence.

It was time Mordecai got to the bottom of Orion IV.

Of course, often as not, the distinction wasn't literal. The underworld could exist in penthouse suites and corporate board rooms as easily as ground-level or even subterranean dwellings. But while organized crime might have been lucrative, Mordecai needed the desperate, terra-grubbing sorts of miscreants to disappear among.

The trick was finding such a place without asking directions.

Five minutes on a tram-stop bench, and Mordecai picked out the worst-dressed pedestrian he could identify amid the masses. Fashion varied from planet to planet, but certain shades of shabbiness were reserved for the downtrodden. Ripped pants and slouching hats came and went from the whims of polite society, but nobody walked around with scuffed shoes as a statement.

Mordecai trailed a slovenly gentleman for twelve blocks before noticing a disreputable chap with a facial scar. He hitched his hopes to that new, dimmer star.

After perhaps a mile, his mark grew suspicious and took evasive maneuvers to lose his shadow. But by then, empty storefronts and graffiti had given Mordecai enough hints that he'd found his part of town.

Whatever the hell town this was.

Rather than stick to streets, he cut through alleys and poked his nose where it least belonged.

"You lost, buddy?"

The voice came from behind him. Before he turned to face the questioner, Mordecai carefully wiped the smile from his face. "As a matter of fact, I am."

Two black-clad, backlit fellows blocked the alley exit behind him. And it appeared that this alley was blind. "What you got in that backpack?"

"If it's money you want, my family is rich."

That much was true. If he dared try to spend money holed up on Earth in various financial labyrinths, Mordecai could have bought whole buildings in this neighborhood.

His two potential assailants swaggered toward him. Only one spoke. "Hand over what you got, maybe we'll give you directions home."

Raising a palm to rub his forehead, Mordecai sighed. "You imbeciles. I'm trying to get kidnapped. Take a goddamn hint."

"What?"

"This guy stimmy or something?" the second shadowy figure finally chimed in.

"Look, have you two got a hover or something? Is it far to your hideout?"

The pair exchanged a worried look. "You a cop or something?"

Mordecai took a step forward and had the satisfaction of the two men retreating to keep their distance. "Oh... much worse." Upturning his free hand, a ball of flame appeared to chase away the gloom. "I'm a wizard looking for a place to crash for the night."

His would-be muggers attempted to run but found their feet frozen to the permacrete.

Unbidden, an idea sprang to mind.

Dropping his pack, Mordecai approached one of his captives, now utterly unable to move. Reaching for the sides of the man's head, he plunged his fingers into the skull as he drank the paltry mind contained within.

The man's companion attempted to scream, but his own mouth was clamped shut to muffle him.

A moment later, a quick fire burned the pair to ash.

Mordecai closed his eyes.

To his surprise, he found himself in a copse of trees surrounding a tiny cottage. His two captives were tied at the wrist and ankle with rope and suspended upside down from a sturdy branch.

"What the bloody—?" he mused before a bellowed greeting caught his attention.

"Mort! There you are, my boy!" Nebuchadnezzar waved as he approached from the cottage's now-open front door. "Wondered when you'd think to check in on me. But when I discovered this delivery of fresh hooligans, I suspected you'd be along shortly. I've put on a kettle for tea."

"Tea?" Mordecai asked incredulously. "I just—"

"Time's quick as a spring hare in here. Been near to fifteen minutes since the first one got here. Despicable sorts. No manners. Far be it from me, not being omnipotent in here, but if you haven't got a reason to keep them around, might I suggest the construction of an oubliette?"

Mordecai clasped his hand behind his back and chewed the inside of his cheek. Sauntering over to his prisoners, he addressed his grandfather. "As a matter of fact, I do have a use for them. I need a guide to a scruffy little corner of Orion IV. And whichever of them does that job best... *doesn't* end up in that oubliette."

Armed with a travel mug of coffee and four hours of sleep, Chuck strolled the morning sights of Crystal Meadows. While it had been the name of a city at the start of his trip, his comedic sensibilities tried to frame it as the stage name of an adult entertainer. Too bad his gigs were family-rated. He had to imagine the locals could sense something was off about their hometown's name; if they couldn't quite tell what that was—and Chuck suspected it was really that there wasn't anything like a meadow planetside on Orion IV—he'd have been happy to fill in the blank.

By core world standards, the air he breathed was fresh and clean. A bite in the wind that gusted down the skyscraper canyons suggested it was local winter in this hemisphere. Not too cold, but just enough to make a guy thankful his wife suggested a jacket before leaving the ship.

If Becky knew why he wanted to stretch his legs at this unmerciful hour, she'd have let him wander off in his boxer shorts.

A quaint copper bell tinkled as Chuck entered a shop called Mysticarium. It was the third shop of its kind he'd found so far, at least by self-description. The first two had been little more than themed joke shops filled with phony wands and costume party wizard robes. They'd had the same bell, like it was code for the unwary shopper. Yet by the pungent, unidentifiable odor upon entry, Chuck suspected this place was different.

Measuring his breathing in case anything was unhealthy in the miasma, Chuck plastered on a smile and sought the proprietor.

"How may I help you, sir?" a nasal voice asked from behind a faux wood counter.

"Got me a minor dilemma. I was hoping you might have what I'm looking for at a price we can both agree on."

The wizard-looking cat working behind the old-timey cash

register looked like someone had made his face out of clay and pinched both the skull and nose a tad too hard. A pair of tiny spectacles that would have been easier to look around than through perched precariously in front of his eyes. "That depends on what you think you'll find here."

Taking a sip of his coffee as much to suck in the aroma as anything, Chuck gestured widely with his free hand. "Lemme lay a story on you. I got myself stranded in the astral a while back—years ago, even. Got it fixed, but it blanked my digits. Keeps happening. One day, I run into a wizard, says the *real* way to travel the astral is bespoke drops by a real live wizard."

The wizard clerk cleared his throat. "Well, it's not unheard of. But no one recommends it; not even the Convocation. Most often, such travel is performed by a ship's star-drive mechanic when a damaged system is preventing an urgent drop."

Chuck waved the idea away. "Forget all that. Humor me. My guy says that you can get around the tech all going dead if you install obsidian rods."

For a moment, the clerk's face froze. "Well. Um. I suppose, technically..."

"What? Is obsidian the wizard equivalent of ivory or tiger nuts or something? What'd I say?"

"I think your friend was having a little fun with you."

"Why? I was just looking to price out what it might cost to set up a family starship... you know, just in case."

If he could just fiddle his way around the tech-deadening aspect of manual astral travel, Chuck could find Mort, bring him back into the fold, and convince Becky to give the fast lane of interstellar travel another chance. "Slow and steady wins the race" would lose out in favor of "crazy fast and dirt cheap."

"Price? Sir, it's not like enchantment-grade obsidian grows on trees, not to mention what it would cost to get someone from the Order of Hephaistos to custom-carve them with the proper runes for the individual starship."

"Slap me a number," Chuck challenged casually. "Total package."

"A quarter million terras."

Chuck's mouth paddled for words before latching onto enough to form a thought. "Who can afford *that*?"

"My point exactly. Emergency astral drops happen, but they accept the technological disruptions. The only ones who gird their vessels against frequent deep astral travel are the Convocation assassin squads—if rumors are to be believed."

This time, Chuck couldn't find anything to say.

Had Mort been joshing him with that line about the obsidian? Was that scrawny vagabond of a wizard actually hinting that he'd need that sort of precaution to stay ahead of his pursuers?

"Forget I mentioned it," Chuck managed when the power of speech returned.

"Of course. Everything said within these walls is in strictest confidence."

Chuck left the shop in a daze. His plan was shot. He wasn't even sure he *wanted* Mort back if he was that hot.

Angling his footsteps in the general direction of the *Radio City*, Chuck ambled through Crystal Meadows lost in thought.

The shop bell rang, and Borland Applebody nearly jumped from his skin. Two gentlemen entered. They wore matching black suits with black dress shirts beneath. Only the Convocation cuff links hinted at their occupation, yet there was no mistaking their intentions by their bearing.

"Wizard Borland?" the one with the salt-and-pepper hair asked.

"Yes-yes-yes. Here. Thank you for coming so quickly." Borland hustled from behind the counter and past his guests, flipping his quaint wooden "OPEN" sign over to "CLOSED" and throwing the deadbolt.

"This man you reported. Can you give a description?"

Borland held up a palm, and an illusory image appeared. It was a human in his middle forties, tall and wide-shouldered but lean, as if he'd been desiccated from a larger specimen. A round face with boyish features and sandy hair sported a grin like a politician. "He came in asking about obsidian rods and talking about a mysterious friend."

"And what did you tell him?"

"Well, at first, I laughed him off. He was clearly a technologist; drinking coffee out of a plastic mug, for Merlin's sake! But he wanted to know how much it would cost to rune-ward a family starship against astral distortion."

"He called it that?"

Borland sniffed. "Of course not. But I could tell that's what he was getting at. I had no galactic idea how much that might cost, so I threw a guess at him and practically broke the dimwit's brain. He asked how anyone could afford such a price... that's when I made the mistake of allowing a revelation past my lips without sufficient contemplation."

"You mentioned the librarians?"

Borland nodded.

The two Convocation agents exchanged a look.

"Do you... do you think this technologist might be involved with... you-know-who?"

The lead agent ignored his question. "When he left here, did you see which way he went?"

"No. Not at all. As soon as he was gone, I went looking for my datapad." Borland held up the device, still caked in dust where he hadn't wiped it from the screen. The gadget had only three comm IDs programmed in. In order, they were labeled: Mom, Layla, and Convocation Tech Liaison's Office. The tech-savvy fellows at the liaison's office had passed the word along.

The second agent spoke his first words since arriving. "Thank you for your time."

Then, the pair headed for the door.

"Would there happen to be—not to put this too bluntly—a reward involved?"

Rumors generally flowed through the Convocation like cold syrup, but this one was making its way through back channels like wildfire. Could the Guardian of the Plundered Tomes be on Orion IV as an outlaw? Borland would be able to sell the shop and retire to Earth. Maybe somewhere in the South Pacific.

"If your information leads to the capture of Mordecai The Brown, we'll make sure your name is mentioned prominently. I'm sure there will be some kind of compensation."

The bell rang again, and the two wizards were gone.

Borland's blood paused a moment to allow him to consider. How long a life could a snitch lead after informing on a Brown? Could he afford security that would protect him from familial retribution, be it from loyalist cousins or a generational feud passed down to his children? Could he ever relax again, retirement or not, sandy beaches or not, terras enough to swim in or not?

Did he want to live his life of luxury dangling by a thread after crossing one of the mystical community's preeminent—and notorious—families?

The bell clanged so hard it might have come loose from its fixture on the wall. Borland shouted after the two Convocation inquisitors, "Don't mention my name!"

Mom was sitting on the couch in front of the holovid. Mike was tucked under her arm, fast asleep. Rhiannon dozed sprawled across her lap. It didn't look like Mom had long before she joined them. With Friendship Bear Squad on series mode, Brad had been subjected to dumb, perky animals bumbling their way through adventure after lame adventure using the power of friendship as an excuse for real conflict.

With Mom's eyes half-glazed and her empty wine glass out of reach, it didn't look like she was going one way or the other quite yet. She teetered on the edge of paying attention to the show and nodding off, succeeding at neither.

This was the mood that doled out answers and agreed to things without thinking them through. Probably not drunk. Definitely not sober. The two kids who couldn't operate a food processor or remember Mom's and Dad's comm IDs were safely wrangled.

Who cared what Brad did?

"Hey, when's Dad getting back?" he asked. It wasn't like Dad wandering off for the better part of a day without telling *Brad* where he was going was all that unusual. But deep down, he was generally pretty sure Mom kept track.

"Who knows?" Mom replied. "He's scrounging for gigs. You know how he gets."

"I'm gonna use your datapad," Brad informed her, picking it up from the side table, where it lay just beside her out-of-reach glass.

"Yeah. Fine," Mom replied absently.

A tiny spark touched dry tinder in Brad's brain. This was a rare mood for Mom, the sweet spot where not only wasn't she paying more than a sleepwalker's attention to what he was saying, she was supplying answers.

A quick detour to his parents' bedroom, and Brad had scrounged up a pair of hundred-terra coins from the stash they thought was secret. On his way back through the living room. "Gonna grab ice cream. Want any change?" He flashed the two coins briefly, quicker than anyone without a slow-mo camera could have checked the denomination.

"I'm fine," Mom replied, stifling a yawn.

The mention of ice cream roused Mike briefly. But after a cursory check to confirm the absence of *actual* ice cream to be had, he nodded back off.

Before anyone could get their act together and ask questions, Brad was off the ship. He slung on his jacket and rolled up the sleeves. The garment only belonged to him on a technicality. It had started life as a castoff, forgotten on a starport bench and taken home by Jamie. When his sister had run off to join Earth Navy, it had gotten left behind.

Brad supposed the navy gave out custom jackets along with the uniform.

Unfortunately, when Brad had outgrown his most recent jacket, Mom had insisted he take this one as his own. But it had been big on Jamie; Brad practically swam in it. Burdened under the clause of "he'll grow into it," he'd been sentenced to cuffing his sleeves and wearing it as a half-trench coat.

Not a good look for a planetside jaunt.

With options that included dying of boredom, freezing to death, or tracking down Dad in an ill-fitting coat, the choice seemed clear.

Whatever had kept Dad away all day had to be better than watching kiddie holovids. He couldn't even hit up Mort for one of those old-timey paper books from his bottomless backpack. Dad could have found a poker game or maybe one of those underground zero-G fighting arenas that allowed betting. He could have been meeting with gangsters to get work in an exclusive nightclub or interviewing wizards to find a replacement for Mort. After all, Dad seemed nutso about free, super-speed astral travel now.

In a way, it was almost better not knowing. Brad always came up with way smoother ideas for stuff that Dad could be doing than what he commonly found.

If Dad was at a poker game, he'd be half drunk and down by more than their docking fees at the starport.

If Dad was negotiating a comedy gig, it would be with some desperate bar owner, not rich gangsters.

Brad had caught his dad scamming shopkeepers and mechanics, selling counterfeit souvenirs to tourists and faking injuries for quick, out-of-court settlements. The only time he could legitimately call his dad's behavior badass was the time he fought off a teenager who tried to pick his pocket—even then, Dad had used brass knuckles to even the odds.

There was always hope for today being better.

Browsing the datapad he shared with his mother, Brad looked up a map of this part of Orion IV. All the best lies wrapped comfortably around a nugget of truth. He really *did* plan to start this journey with some ice cream. Going by the ratings on DinnerBlab, there was a great racing-themed creamery right on the borderline between the Port North District where the *Radio City* was parked and nearby Crystal Meadows.

He had the hardcoin to take a cab, but anything he didn't

spend he planned to keep. At the risk of blowing up to a quarter of what he'd stolen from Mom, he chose to hoof it.

When the datapad chimed, he checked the message by reflex. Who cared if it was for Mom? Since when had that ever stopped him?

The message was from Dad. At the risk of potentially spoiling his adventure, he read it.

Being held hostage.

They'll trade me for the wizard.

You know how this works.

Dad hadn't even signed off with any of his puke-inducing flirty one-liners he kept trying on Mom.

This was serious.

Or it was a more elaborate joke than usual from Dad.

Either way, there was only one thing to be done.

Tapping quickly, Brad shot back a reply.

I can swing it.

Where and when?

Only dipshits hassled kidnappers. The smart move was always giving them what they wanted.

As Brad set off on a new mission to find Mort God-only-knew-where on Orion IV, his worries about Dad's safety hid behind a cynical smirk.

None of them knew a whole lot about Mort. But Brad was pretty sure whoever wanted to meet him so bad wasn't ready for who they were dealing with.

Chuck flexed his hands but found his wrists held tight. While the utilitarian dining-room chair wasn't what he'd have called comfortable, it was far from the worst chair he'd ever been tied to. Not that, in the strictest sense, he was tied to this one. Rather, the arms of the chair had grown iron shackles out of their painted plastic surface and shrunken them to fit without room to slip a toothpick between metal and skin.

Near as he could tell, he was being held on the fifth floor of a vacant retail building. The grimy floor had clean spots with crisp, defined outlines where counters and display cases had been removed. Utility panels flopped open, and cables for data and power slithered across the floor like beheaded snakes, connected to nothing.

Out the full-wall front window, aerial traffic buzzed against the backdrop of a productive city going about its oblivious business. Chuck had to imagine that no one could see in through the glassteel, otherwise someone on a core world like Orion IV ought to have called the cops by now.

He shared the room with his three captors. None of them had identified themselves by name. To him they'd become Mr. Grim, Mr. Creepy, and The Weenie. The first two had to have been wizards due to simple logic. When they'd pulled Chuck off the street, Mr. Grim had claimed to be a Convocation inquisitor. And while that might have potentially been a lie, Mr. Creepy had produced a small ball of flame in the palm of his hand and not contradicted his partner's claim.

The Weenie was the youngest of the three and had been fiddling nonstop with Chuck's datapad since confiscating it.

"We're going to ask you again," Mr. Grim said. "Have you seen this man?" He kept a palm upturned, and like a manual holo-projector, a perfect likeness of Mort floated before Chuck's eyes. When he didn't answer, the wizard snapped, "HAVE YOU SEEN HIM?"

Cringing back as far as he could in the chair, Chuck painted on his best look of incredulous innocence. "Hwhy you heff to be mad?" he asked in reply, using a phony accent he'd practiced for a bit he'd cobbled together from the Russo-American Ice War. "Is just man on road. Heff not seen heem before today."

"Where?"

"What did he say to you about astral travel?" Mr. Creepy put in.

Given the choice, and needing to string these bozos along, Chuck opted for the simpler question from the angrier interrogator. "On road. Over..." He grunted and wiggled a finger. "There. Ken't point."

"Aha!" The Weenie cheered from the corner. "I got it."

Mr. Grim diverted his attention to the guy waving Chuck's datapad triumphantly. "Does it say who he is?"

The Weenie scanned the screen, swiped, tapped, swiped some more. "Yeah. We've got ourselves one Boris Sukavich Badenov, native of Argos VI."

Mr. Grim broke character and smirked. "Find whatever you can from that infernal device. Meanwhile... Mr. Badenov—"

"Pleece, coll me Boris," Chuck replied with casual familiarity.

He'd paid good money to join ID-Swapper. They'd better have kept Boris's comm logs up to date. Chuck hadn't bothered to swap to the alternate profile on his datapad and make misleading comms himself.

"Boris," Mr. Grim clarified. "We have an eyewitness who saw you in the company of Mordecai The Brown. Wizard Mordecai is Convocation Enemy Number One. Do you understand what I'm saying?"

"Em speeking the Eenglish, em I not?"

Gritting his teeth, Mr. Grim leaned in close. "We're not

playing games here. You're going to tell us everything you know about Mordecai The Brown, or we're going to start—"

"Hokay... hokay," Chuck replied hurriedly, mentally shifting his weight from the "stall" to "cooperate" on the teeter-totter he was stranded atop over a pit of fire. "Geef dataped. I send comm. Friend breeng wizard."

Mr. Creepy turned to The Weenie. "Can we trust him with that doodad?"

"No," The Weenie admitted. "But I can watch over his shoulder. If he tries anything... well, I probably can't stop him in time, but you've certainly convinced him of the price he'd pay."

Chuck strained to reach for the device, feebly stretching his fingers to grab it from five meters across the room. "You geef. I send. No problem."

After a considerable pause while a scowl deepened on his brow, Mr. Grim gave a curt nod. "Hand it to him."

One of the shackles receded with a wave of Mr. Creepy's hand. The Weenie tossed the datapad onto Chuck's lap and watched over him as he tapped in a comm to an ID he'd really hoped to keep out of this mess.

In an ideal world, the ID would have confused these clowns and muddied the waters of whether he was really the guy they were looking for. They hadn't even scanned the doctored left thumbprint that would have connected to the alternate identity.

To put it bluntly, the Convocation was too low tech to buy his alias. They had an eyewitness, and that was that.

And so, Chuck punched in Becky's comm ID and hoped that she could bail him out of this somehow.

Being held hostage.

They'll trade me for the wizard.

You know how this works.

Mordecai bustled around the apartment, torn between focusing on his plans and a general irritation with the squalor in which his captive had lived. Between the two of them, this was the larger and more centrally located domicile. Its former inhabitant, a cretin by the name of Laurent Drudge, held no shred of shame over the filth and grime, the disrepair, or the incriminating stolen goods piled in the closet or shoved beneath the bed.

Still, it was better than the alternative, bunking with Sterling Bono's mother and older sister the next district over.

Mordecai had done the pair a favor killing them. What they'd experienced since... well, that might have been less a favor, but it had gotten the wizard all the information he needed to find this place and operate the keypad to unlock it without drawing attention to his magic.

Two small rubbish depots cluttered the kitchen table. One was the remnants of Szechuan takeout, at least a day old by the smell. The other was a work in progress as Mordecai made his way through a family-sized order of curried ramen from a roving neighborhood vendor.

Footsore and numb to the soul, Mordecai used his chopsticks to lift noodles to his mouth paying scant attention to the process. Eyes unfocused, he plotted his next move.

Orion IV wasn't his card game. It was more of a whist, while Mordecai was a poker kind of wizard. Even finding this sorry excuse of a pseudo-slum had been arduous, and it was still the kind of place where transient noodle peddlers plied their trade without a hint of fear.

Too big. Too connected. Too... scientific.

A low-rent independent knuckle-man like Laurent Drudge had a techno-lock on his door and a toilet that required ten minutes of fiddling to figure out how to flush. There wasn't a book in the place nor a scrap of artwork on the walls. Mordecai hadn't attempted to activate the small pedestal that conjecture held was probably a holo-projector.

In the back of Mordecai's mind, a worry sucked at his resolve like a tick.

Was there anyplace in the galaxy where he belonged? Anyplace besides Earth?

Thoughts of Nancy and the kids nagged. Mordecai's criminal behavior must have come to light by now, casting his family into the considerable shadow of his actions. What must they be saying about him? Would they connect him to Nebuchadnezzar's death? Did they know even half the vile secrets contained in the *Tome of Bleeding Thoughts*? How wide a net had Wenling dragged over his life, and who had been caught up in it?

A knock at the door perked Mordecai's ears and sped his blood. Jamming his chopsticks into a tangle of noodles, he got up and crept over to the door. Laurent hadn't been expecting visitors. Mordecai most certainly wasn't.

Flame leapt to Mordecai's hand with nary a thought, held at the ready to incinerate whoever might wait beyond that door. His unexpected guest might have half a second to appear contrite and nonthreatening before they spent the remainder of that second experiencing their horrific death.

Forming his free hand into a claw, Mordecai played a quick round of charades with the universe and tore open the door with magic.

"Hi," Bradley said with a wave and a tight smile.

Closing his fist, Mordecai extinguished the flame. Grabbing the boy by the wrist, Mordecai yanked him inside, then slammed shut the door behind them.

"What are you doing here? And how did you find me?"

"My dad's in trouble." He held out a datapad, but the screen was blank. When Mordecai didn't react to the inert device, Bradley examined it briefly. "Shit. It was there a second ago."

"Let it be," Mordecai advised. "Usually temporary."

Bradley shrugged. "'Kay. Anyway, finding you was easy."

Mordecai's hot blood chilled. "It was?"

"Sure. I just asked around."

"Asked around?" Mordecai echoed, sounding like an idiot even to himself. However, if this information proved to be true, it violated a presumption on his part—namely that people in these sorts of low-law areas didn't answer questions about strangers.

"Sure," Bradley replied with a shrug. "I gave your description, told people you were my father, and that I couldn't comm you because I was trying to bring you your datapad."

"And nobody just gutted you and stole the datapad?"

Bradley smirked. "It's the one Mom and I share. It's like a million years old. Only a square would use it. Besides, I'm a kid. I know how to recognize the ones who draw the line at roughing up a kid."

Such wisdom packaged in a body too young to hold it. Bright-eyed cynicism, Nebuchadnezzar had called it, except he'd been referring to Mordecai when he was a lad. Open acceptance of the galaxy as a shitty place and the savvy to operate within it as such.

"Aha!" Bradley cheered, then presented the datapad again.

It was along the lines of a ransom note without quite being one. The words danced around certain question words and nuance that undoubtedly lay below the surface. He also saw the pithy reply.

Mordecai turned the problem over in his head.

Clearly, someone had apprehended Chuck Ramsey as a witness. In isolation, Mordecai could have written that off as someone operating at the edge of legality running afoul of local police. But legitimate law enforcement didn't make trades like that and certainly weren't interested in wizards—quite the opposite. That meant the Convocation had taken Chuck.

That his captors hadn't probed Chuck's mind for the answers they needed suggested middling agents at work. No legal barrier prevented such mental incursion, so it had to have been lack of ability. Sending a comm hinted that either these were tech-literate wizards or had help from a tech liaison. The latter hinted at institutional awareness and support; the former would have been a blessing; Mordecai doubted the existence of a wizard who could both operate a datapad and pose a threat to him.

Sending the comm also meant that they expected Chuck meant something to him.

A leap of logical faith to be sure. Hinted at desperation.

Bradley kept quiet as Mordecai pondered, watching him with eyes that must have been hiding a similar self-conversation within his own skull.

"What do you think is going on?" he asked the boy. Bradley had proved himself competent in these dusty-moralled dealings. Maybe a youthful and technologically savvy perspective might cast new light over an unfamiliar landscape.

"Dad got nabbed. Can't quite say how, but if I had to

guess, maybe he was looking for a way to buy those odd sibbian rods you told him about."

Mordecai furrowed his brow. "Obsidian," he corrected. "It's a black volcanic stone. And what makes you say that?" It was beneath him to scold the boy for eavesdropping at this point. His instincts for skullduggery were the only reason Mordecai had consulted the boy.

"Mom won't let us go bitchin' fast if it makes the ship black out. You told Dad those volcano stones could fix it. That's how Dad thinks. Got a problem? Come up with a plan to fix it. He doesn't give up."

Still scowling, Mordecai shook his head. "Still doesn't make any sense. He'd still need to find a wizard to install them and join the crew to perform the magic. Where was he planning on finding another wizard?"

While astral drops weren't exactly legend-of-Merlin feats of spell craft, he might have left the comedian with an unrealistic view of the caliber of wizard it might take to fill such a role on his vessel. More than half the Convocation were dilettantes barely able to finagle the half-technological star-drives into working order. And that percentage was galaxy-wide; most of the wizards who could find proper work in magical fields were based out of Earth.

"Duh?" Bradley replied sarcastically. "His plan was to find *you*."

Mordecai's face went slack. "He just sent me away. Why would he want me back?"

"He sent you away because Mom made him. I was listening through a door. Was he—I dunno—winking or something?"

Scratching just above his temple, Mordecai struggled to

recall. "Couldn't say. Wasn't exactly trying to suss out ulterior motives. I've got a lot else on my mind of late."

Bradley smiled. "He likes you. You're fun."

"I'm fun?" Now Mordecai had completely lost the thread of logic at work.

"Yeah. Regular people are boring. You tell funny stories, use words *nobody* else uses, and you don't make fun of his jokes."

Mordecai swallowed, mouth having gone dry. "You… you know I'm on the run from the law—wizard law, that is—don't you?"

Bradley shrugged. "Most of Dad's friends are criminals. Mom won't let most of them on the ship. But she let you once. If we can get Dad back, maybe she will again."

Glyphs of an unknown and incomprehensible language came into focus in clear English for the first time.

"This is *your* plan to get me back on the *Radio City*, isn't it?"

Bradley looked away. "You can have the bottom bunk. When it's just me, I remember when Jamie slept there."

"Who's Jamie?"

"My sister."

"You mean Rhiannon." Mordecai hadn't forgotten the names of his hosts' kids so readily. Bradley, Michael, Rhiannon. Three children, ages 12, 4, and 2.

"Jamie is the oldest. She got mad at Mom and Dad. They always used to fight. Something about her eyndar boyfriend. Anyway, she joined Earth Navy. They don't talk about her anymore."

Mordecai rested a hand on Bradley's shoulder and bent down to his level. "Brad, I can't replace your sister."

Shrugging off both his maudlin mood and Mordecai's

hand, the boy snapped, "No shit, Mort. But since you came aboard is the happiest anyone's been since she left—except Rhiannon; she barely remembers Jamie."

"What would you have me do? Trade myself for your father?" Several scenarios occurred to him wherein he might escape custody after such an exchange.

It was the boy's turn to scowl. "No. You're like some rogue wizard hunter, right?"

Mordecai recalled couching his profession more vaguely than that, but the boy was shrewd, after all. He nodded his reply. "But these aren't dark wizards?"

Bradley folded his arms. "Paradigm shift."

Despite the circumstances, Mordecai got a chuckle out of hearing the boy spout such a philosophical context. "What paradigm?"

"You think people are good or bad. You think laws are laws. Dad always said that everyone's an outlaw in their heart. Laws are for scaredy-cats. You do what *you* think is right." He ticked off on his fingers. "Family, friends, community, society. Unless you're rich, you can't afford to worry past friends on that list. Society doesn't care about you. If you're on the move, no community even knows you. All that matters are family and friends."

Wizards could have minds as hard as diamond and just as unyielding. All the great wizards possessed a unique ability to change not only the universe around them but their own beliefs as well. Could Mordecai The Brown, Guardian of the Plundered Tomes, exist outside the paradigm of the Convocation?

As Mordecai considered the consequences, Bradley fiddled on his datapad.

"What are you up to, boy?"

Bradley ignored him for several seconds, then showed a pair of messages on the screen.

Got him. Where/when?

Followed by...

Greely Building. Fifth floor. No surprises.

"How does an outlaw handle this sort of thing?"

Bradley grinned. The boy knew he was hooked. "If you're facing a stronger foe, you come up with a trick or a distraction, then free the prisoner in the chaos. The Switcheroo, the Bowler Hat Brigade, the Goodyear Blimp, Inflatable Army, Friends With Bullhorn Fits."

"Which one would *we* use?"

"None of the above. You," Bradley poked him in the chest, "are a badass. You're going to march in there, knock some heads around, and *get my dad back*!"

Wenling sat at the desk in her home office, barricaded behind stacks of reports. The room smelled of fresh parchment and barely dry ink. Though she had yet to admit her error in judgment, she resisted rescinding her order to bring all reports on the Wizard Mordecai matter to her personal attention.

The sheer volume of flotsam through which to pick had her yearning for the days of pliable graduate students eager to do her bidding. Since giving the order to personally oversee all the Grand Council's intelligence on the search, her inquisitorial staff had proved to be only too eager to divest themselves of the minutiae.

A knock at the door preceded its opening before she had time to grant permission to enter. Lisa Smithers from the tech liaison's office strode in, datapad held out before her like a jouster's lance. "Ma'am, we have a confirmed sighting."

"Confirmed?" the chief inquisitor echoed. "Where?" Her mind raced ahead, predicting guesses. Greece seemed most likely. Someone in the Order of Prometheus might have harbored him. Or perhaps Egypt. Multiple unconfirmed reports had someone matching the description of Mordecai The Brown lurking in the tourist enclave near the Great Pyramid of Giza.

"A team on Orion IV has an eyewitness in custody and is bartering with a technologist family who gave him transport."

Questions danced at her lips, but Wenling withheld them. Instead, she snatched the datapad from the young liaison's grasp and perused the missive for herself. The details were sketchy, nothing that would have held weight for a warrant on Earth. But this wasn't the kind of investigation that waited on warrants, and it wasn't taking place on Earth.

"What do we know about this Badenov character?" Wenling demanded.

"Nothing yet, ma'am," Lisa replied as she lowered her gaze. "They're seeking permission to enlist reinforcements."

Wenling tapped a fingernail to her lip. Mordecai was beyond shrewd. Devious barely did him justice. The plan already relied on the subterfuge of amateurs and technophiles to lure the Guardian of the Plundered Tomes into a trap. The more wizards on site, the better the chance of him seeing the trap before it was too late.

Then, Wenling allowed her gaze to wander to a separate pile on her desk—research on her adversary. Mostly, it consisted of copied records of his plundering activities. Previously, his exploits had served to merely spice the daily tedium of council meetings. This dark wizard or that one was no longer a threat to the Convocation at large. A listing of new volumes for the Plundered Tomes occasionally contained an unsettling glimpse into the mind of madness.

Now, she saw the factual accountings of those clashes. Dark wizards didn't simply *cease* being a threat. Someone had to cease them. Manually. Personally. Permanently.

Three names floated among the details of this sighting on Orion IV. The tech liaison who'd compiled it drifted at the edge of familiarity. Possibly an aunt or grandmother who had worked in the liaison's office on Earth a few decades ago. But the two wizards on site were unknown to her, which meant they were nobodies, too far down the hierarchy to warrant anything more than a summary approval of new recruits vetted and trained by distant underlings.

They stood no chance. The rule of two wills against one would do nothing this time.

"Afford them all the backup available. Commendations for any involved in successfully subduing Mordecai The Brown."

"Yes, ma'am," Lisa acknowledged with a curt bow before rushing off to deliver the order.

Wenling contemplated a ceremony wherein she presented medals to a line of wizards resembling an Olympic track and field team.

She hoped there were enough wizards to assemble such a team in time.

Mordecai hustled down the street with his young guide in tow. The lad had good legs under him and kept up with an adult pace without complaint. An occasional shout from behind him gave Mordecai their next turn in the maze of irregular streets and decorative signage that did more to mislead than to give navigational help.

While the lad thought they were off on a grand adventure, Mordecai knew better. This was a trap. It had to be. No one in their right mind shouted their location at the top of their lungs —or digital letters in this case—without a plan to exploit the one arriving.

How clever were his adversaries? Left with his thoughts, Mordecai considered a deeper layer of strategy.

Chuck didn't know a damn thing. Mordecai could have disappeared into the throngs inhabiting Orion IV or already booked passage to the border colonies for all the comedian knew. If his captors *had* cracked into the man's mind to peer around, they might have feigned ignorance of the contents in order to lure a suspicious wizard into merely *thinking* they lacked the willpower to do so.

Checkmate. Mordecai would be trapped by one or more competent wizards, certainly strong enough to contest against the notorious Guardian of the Plundered Tomes. After all, why else would anyone be bothering unless they *knew* who they were dealing with.

Conversely, Mordecai could avoid this whole mess by disguising some poor slob as him, marching him off to the exchange, and letting the wizards think their informant had been wrong. That would make Chuck Ramsey superfluous. If these were decent, by-the-book wizards, they'd scrub his memory a little and turn him loose.

If.

A small word on which to hang the hopes of the amiable comedian's life.

There was the alternative, of course. Chuck might have given Mordecai up and been cooperating with the

Convocation. He certainly knew enough to aid them, even if his help would be marginal. Merely approaching the Convocation to report him on Orion IV would have been a devastating betrayal when those hash-smokers back on Earth would think he was still on the same planet as them.

"Left at the next intersection," Bradley called out.

"Right," Mordecai muttered as he crossed land traffic consisting of low-altitude grav vehicles and pedestrians.

There was simply no knowing for sure unless he got there. If he took Bradley's information and paved footprints off this colony, he'd be jumping at rumors the rest of his life. He had to take the fight to his pursuers, or they'd eventually come to the conclusion that harassing Mordecai The Brown didn't carry any consequences.

He had to know for sure, and "sure" meant firsthand.

A hand caught him by the sleeve. "Wait. That's it."

Bradley leaned around the corner of a daycare center and pointed to a building across the street. Mordecai looked the boy over. Those keen eyes studied the building as if *he* were the one about to potentially launch an assault on whoever lay in wait within.

If it was Chuck... I'll look after him, he promised himself. There was a sense of cosmic balance in the idea of taking himself from his own children for their protection and taking the place of Chuck Ramsey when he could no longer care for his boy.

Let Becky keep the little ones. Two parents couldn't keep Bradley under control, let alone one of them solo. Mordecai would take this lad in... maybe make a wizard of him.

But he was getting ahead of himself.

"What's the plan?" Bradley asked eagerly.

Mordecai slung the pack off his shoulder and pressed it

into the boy's arms. "Hold this. Don't go digging inside or something might drag you in. I'll be right back."

With that, Mordecai The Brown cracked his knuckles and crossed the street.

▭

Chuck slouched in his chair as best his trapped wrists would allow. The posture alleviated some of the pressure on a bladder on the verge of exploding. As a shrewd judge of human nature, he pegged his captors for the sort who'd rather have him piss himself than allow him a washroom break.

"Thees take much longker? I heff places to be," he complained. The more firmly he could lodge Boris Badenov in these narcs' minds, the less likely they'd be to stumble across any signs of a Chuck Ramsey. Becky would get this cleared up.

Or maybe she'd find the wizard. Mort would speak these jokers' language.

Either way, his missive was off in the digital realm, doing work. Anyone willing to live in the gray spaces of the law knew that starting *after* you got captured was a script for a community theater rescue plan. The smart scofflaw kept contingencies, favors, and hidden stashes squirreled away for a day like this.

Any minute now, that elevator door would open. Chuck pictured the scene to keep his spirits up.

INTERIOR - ABANDONED HAIR SALON

(Chuck had finally placed the whiff in the air as a combination of laser-trimmed hair and ladies' conditioning foam.)

Elevator doors part. The wizards gawk. Enter Thuggy

McNoneck, wearing a thousand-terra business suit with a suspicious bulge betraying a shoulder-holstered blaster.

THUGGY: What are you doing with my friend Chuck here?

Well, the jig would be up at that point, but Chuck smirked at the flabbergasted realizations that Chuck had friends in low places. There would be haggling, discussions of consequences and who knew whom, local jurisdiction, and all that jazz. Eventually, Thuggy would casually slip in a personal detail like where one of the wizards' kids went to school or the tech guy's debts to a certain illicit casino, and a deal would get hashed out.

"What's so funny?" Mr. Grim snapped. He'd been pacing the past hour, while Mr. Creepy sat cross-legged on the floor by the window as he sipped coffee and kept watch.

"Theenking joke I hear at komedy show. Ya? Good one. You like."

It was the first thing that came to mind, and Chuck dreaded the answer. Sure, maybe these guys wouldn't credit Boris with sufficient language skills to recount the bit. However, given the anxiety flooding the room like Venice Prime during tourist season, they just might be bored enough to take him up on the offer.

"Shut up," Mr. Creepy ordered. "And you, just ignore him."

The Weenie perked up, however. "I wouldn't mind hearing—"

With a ding, the elevator arrived. Doors opened. No brute with syndicate ties stepped out. Instead, three guys and one gal in baggy-sleeved suits marched into the room, followed by a bald dude in datagoggles.

"What's the status?" one of the new wizards demanded.

Unlike the work-a-day bozos who'd been holding him prisoner, this wizard had an air of authority same as if he'd been wearing a crown. "Any word on the arrival of Mordecai The Brown?"

Paying attention to the other three additional wizards, Chuck picked up on the tension. Tight shoulders, shallow breathing, wide pupils. These narcs were scared.

"We have confirmation of an exchange in..." Mr. Grim drew out the word, seeking a rescue of his own.

"Eighteen minutes," The Weenie chimed in helpfully.

"And you're sure he's being delivered and not using this time to make his escape?" the newcomer asked, whom Chuck tentatively named King Wizard.

"Of course not," Mr. Grim shot back with a scowl. "But it's our current plan. If you've got the resources to cast a net over the planet without involving local police, I'm all for it."

King Wizard let the matter drop and took charge, touring the vacant space as if it were a military camp. "Simple plan. We overwhelm and suppress. No magic. I want everyone's complete focus on maintaining the scientific paradigm. Six is overkill, but this is Mordecai The Brown. I'm comfortable with overkill and splitting the credit six ways."

Chuck blinked, still hung up on wizards talking about maintaining science. They could do that? It seemed like everyone thought they were the exact opposite of science.

"It's staying at six," Goggles reported. "Stubens and Stroyga are two hours out, stuck on public transit. No one else is any closer."

"Six is more than enough," King Wizard confirmed. "I'm more worried that we're all being made fools of. This the informant?"

The Weenie swept a hand toward Chuck. "Meet Boris Badenov. Apparently Wizard Mordecai put him up to shopping for astral-grade obsidian. That means our target is looking for a fast ride off Orion."

"'Our' target?" Mr. Creepy echoed. "As if you won't be hiding in a corner when he shows up."

"Hey, you guys hold his magic in check, I'll help you wrestle him to the floor."

This was all fascinating. Chuck hadn't given much thought to wizard battles before today, but he pictured fire and lightning, demons boiling from cracks in the ground, that sort of thing. This was all sounding like an after-school fight with a bully by the bicycle rack.

Stomping footsteps sounded from behind the emergency exit stairwell. All eyes in the room turned to watch the door.

"On your guard, everyone!" King Wizard ordered in a loud whisper.

The door flung open, and a puffing, panting Mort stood there. "Egad! Why can't they make a wizard-friendly elevator?"

King Wizard drew himself tall and leveled a finger like a fencer's saber toward Mort. "Seize him!"

Winded and annoyed, it didn't take long for Mordecai to take stock of the situation. A vacant office of some sort, akin to the corpse of a technological beast, filled with Convocation stooges of the lowest sort. Wizardly presences radiated with a stubborn insistence that the laws of physics resist all attempts to obey the whimsy of anyone else's magic. Six of them, by quick count. That left two datapad-lugging nobodies from the local tech liaison's office.

And Chuck.

The comedian sat shackled to a pathetic chair, the lone piece of furniture in the room. Had the rest of them *stood* there waiting for him? What kind of idiots were these? All the same sort, or had he stumbled onto a variety pack?

"Seize him!" the one obviously in charge shouted, aiming a finger in case his lackeys might have seized in the wrong direction without visual aids.

"How much you tell these guys?" Mort yelled past the clumsy charge of bumbling academics pressed into law enforcement duty. He had time to decide what needed to be done here.

While the fates of the Convocation contingent were sealed, he needed to know how much collateral damage had been done. Was the *Radio City* made? While the initial comm had suggested Chuck hadn't been cooperating beyond what they already knew, had they broken his mind in the meantime?

"Run, Mort!" Chuck warned. "It's a trap! They've got you outnumbered!"

No shit, they had the numbers advantage. There was only one of him. Unless someone had half a wizard lying around somewhere, he'd find no better than even odds in any fight for the rest of his life.

He felt the pressure, the insistent wills that sided with science and the technological mindset for the time being. In a contest of equals, two wizards could hold one another's magic entirely in check if that was all they tried. Two on one swung the balance in all but the most lopsided cases.

"Stop," Mordecai ordered without raising his voice.

The tentative, halfhearted charge faltered. And why not? He wasn't trying to run or make a mad dash for their prisoner or even lift his feet from their spots on the floor.

From the back of his mind, a tiny, familiar old crotchety voice egged him on. *I've got your back. Get 'em!*

Turning his thoughts briefly inward, Mordecai fired back. *Zip it, Gramps. You're the reason I'm here in the first place.*

With a final few deep breaths, Mordecai regained his wind. Before he could speak, the wizard in charge blustered at him.

"By order of the Convocation Grand Council, you are hereby charged with—"

"Silence!" Mordecai thundered. He spread his hands. "This is an insult! I am Mordecai The Fucking Brown, Oxford Valedictorian, descendant of Merlin himself, and Guardian of the Plundered Tomes. Where does the Convocation get off sending the Princeton Junior Varsity Debate Team to arrest me?"

One of the younger wizards raised a finger. "I actually attended—"

"It's a kill order," the leader cut in before Mordecai could sap the willpower of the enemy any further. "And your little tricks to make my colleagues doubt themselves won't work. Kneel, and at least die with some dignity." He drew a thin knife from a sheath tucked lengthwise behind his belt.

The willpower of the six wizards had indeed ebbed during Mordecai's speech, but it buoyed itself rapidly.

"Trick?" Mort scoffed. "I'm genuinely offended. And if there's one thing I've learned—and there are certainly more than one—it's that death has no dignity. But it *can* be either quick or agonizing. I'll give you boys—and girl—a choice. Let my casual acquaintance go, and I'll make it the quick version."

The lead wizard glanced around at his underlings. None of them were making a move. "What are you waiting for? He's bluffing! It's his only chance and he knows it!"

In a ragged infantry charge, the wizards rushed him.

With a snap of his fingers all six of them burst into flame. Their screams filled the office as Mordecai stepped aside to avoid their flailing and thrashing as they attempted to extinguish magical flames that could have burned under water.

"Don't hurt us!" the bald tech in the goggles begged. He held up both palms and backed toward the full-length window. "We can't do anything."

Mordecai advanced slowly on the pair. "Truer words..." He left the rest unspoken. "Fair enough. I won't hurt you. But since I can't have you spreading knowledge of my whereabouts and associates—"

Tapping the air with an index finger from each hand, the two tech liaisons crumbled to ash.

"But you said..." Chuck babbled.

"They didn't feel a thing," Mordecai promised. "Plus, it was either them or you. Come on." He dissolved the shackles and offered the comedian a hand getting up.

"Damn, have I gotta piss."

Mordecai looked down at the wizards still moaning on the floor in helpless agony as Promethean Fire slowly consumed them. "Knock yourself out. It won't extinguish the flames."

"Um... a washroom maybe?"

Mordecai huffed a sigh. "Yeah. I saw a sign on the way up."

"Glad Becky found you. I was hoping not to call in my other favor."

"Wasn't Becky," Mordecai informed him as they bypassed the tech-dead elevator and ducked into the stairwell. "That boy of yours is all right in my book."

Dinner at the Pao household had been unusually quiet. The servants had been on tiptoe since delivering the dessert course. Solomon had made an attempt at conversation early in the meal but had quickly caught on that Wenling was in no mood this evening.

Through the terrace window, sunset hung over Boston Prime.

As Wenling lifted the last bite of crème brûlée to her mouth, the door to the kitchen opened. Larkspur entered, bearing a silver platter and cloche.

"This arrived just now, madame," the butler announced with a curtsy before lifting the cloche to reveal a datapad.

Setting down her spoon, Wenling accepted the missive and nodded her dismissal. "Thank you, Larkspur."

"What news?" Solomon asked with a craned neck, pantomiming a desire to peer over the top. As if he could read it from the far end of a table that sat forty.

Larkspur hadn't moved.

"You may go."

"Madame, they requested a reply."

With a sigh, Wenling relented and allowed the butler to remain as she read.

Dessert curdled in her stomach the farther through the message she progressed.

"Something amiss, Butterfly?" Solomon asked cautiously.

She shook the datapad. "Our esteemed colleagues on Orion IV report that Mordecai has disappeared utterly. No trace. No leads. They lost four inquisitors, two local peacekeepers, and a pair of tech liaisons in the process." Addressing Larkspur, she added. "Who brought this?"

"He's waiting in the foyer, madame. From the liaison's office. He didn't leave a name."

"Send him in."

"Sweetums, couldn't this wait until after—"

"No," Wenling snapped. "It cannot."

She set down the datapad and dabbed at the corners of her mouth with a napkin. By the time the liaison arrived, she was straight-backed and scowling, crushing the man under a withering gaze his entire trip through the dining room.

The liaison was neither young nor old, occupying an indeterminate middle ground that could have boasted of 25 years or 40 without raising eyebrows. His beard was neatly trimmed, and he kept his hands in his sleeves respectfully despite a snowstorm's chance on Venus of working magic in *her* presence. However, by the cut of his sleeves, it suggested he wasn't a tech himself, merely a tech-capable wizard—a would-be star-drive tinkerer who'd found gainful employment in a respectable occupation.

It occurred to Wenling that she'd probably been introduced to him at some point but couldn't have deigned to retain his name.

"Chief Inquisitor," he greeted her with a bow.

"Those nincompoops on Orion, upon discovering the arrival of a volcano in their midst, chose to investigate it by leaping into the lava."

"As you say, Chief Inquisitor. I don't read them; just deliver them. Wizard Herodotus was quite eager for a reply indicating how his people ought to proceed in this matter."

That name, at least, sang a full song in her mind. Herodotus Eastman had taken over the Convocation Outreach Center in the Orion system. The man was responsible for three inhabited planets and a variety of moons, totaling in excess of twelve hundred wizards of varying specializations.

If he'd been any good, he'd have stayed on Earth.

"Yes, I have instructions for Wizard Herodotus." A twitch of two fingers lifted the datapad to float untouched through the air, drifting gently toward the liaison's waiting hands.

Halfway there, the device flickered and went blank. A split second later, the plastic glowed a molten red. As the liaison yelped and backed away, the datapad melted to a smoking puddle on the Pao Estate's marble dining room floor.

"You will inform Wizard Herodotus that his people are to report anything about Mordecai The Brown to my office immediately. Any direct action against the *former* Guardian of the Plundered Tomes will be considered unauthorized and punished as such. I will *not* have my inquisitors wasted on vain efforts to apprehend a wizard so far above their pay grade."

"As you command, Chief Inquisitor." The liaison bowed and backed toward the door.

She wasn't done with him yet. "One more thing. Get messages to the first chair and bursar. I wish to confer with them at their earliest convenience."

While she could order nearly anyone else around, two of her fellow councilors had to at least be afforded the luxury of pretending she'd accept waiting for their schedules to clear.

When they were alone again, Solomon rekindled the embers of a conversation. "Shall I have Larkspur fetch wine while you fill me in on everything you're planning?"

Wine did sound good. He'd known her nearly fifty years and was the only one able to read her moods. "I'll drink with you, but I'm afraid I'll have the story finished before the bottle's uncorked."

"Do tell?" Fifteen years her elder, Solomon could still provoke an unguarded giggle from her with a waggle of his eyebrows.

"Mordecai The Brown is making fools of us and will no

doubt continue to do so. Thus, I intend to place a bounty on his head so high they'll write poems about him one day."

"Not exactly the way to keep this matter quiet."

"I'm through with quiet. I just want him dead."

By the following evening, word had spread throughout the magical community of Earth. The Times London quoted anonymous sources within Convocation investigative circles. Self-proclaimed sages penned open editorials. The circus had come to Boston Prime, and the clowns were holding a parade with Mordecai The Brown as ringmaster *in absentia.*

"Mommy, when's Daddy coming home?" Cedric asked, tugging at the bottom of Nancy's evening edition of The Times London.

Nancy sensed the willpower at work, attempting to burn the newsprint that barred the boy's view of his mother. With practiced stubbornness, she stamped down on the mystical forces brewing in a child too young to be so full of himself.

It ran in the blood, they said.

If Nancy had known years ago just how true that old saying rang, she'd have married a terramancer. She could live with kids trying to divert the back garden fountains through a canyon carved in the sand box or growing miniature oaks in their bedrooms.

Cassie had learned. She had the temperament of an oracle despite the fires of Hades itself burning in her veins. If only Cedric would follow suit before he grew stronger than her.

All the same, she couldn't ignore the question that vexed him so. Neither, she believed down to her bones, could she feed these children sweet lies until it rotted their trust in her. "I don't expect that Daddy will be coming home at all."

"But I want Daddyyyyyyyyyyyyyyyyyyyyy!" Cedric wailed, stomping his feet and turning beet red in the face as he attempted to burn the house down around all of them. Luckily, the tipping point where he stood any chance of succeeding while Nancy had anything to say about it was years off. Hopefully, by then he'd be off to boarding school where sterner masters of the mystic arts could hold his tantrums in check.

Or, she supposed, he might outgrow them.

"The girls at bowling practice said that Daddy's a bad guy," Cassie interjected casually. "I told Artemis that if she ever said it again, I'd break her nose with one of the big balls with finger holes."

"Don't bluster, dear," Nancy corrected the girl reflexively, speaking with Mort's voice more so than her own. Next, she'd be telling her daughter to either break the girl's nose or not; forewarning being the provenance of blowhards. "And don't go around fighting with your friends. Attack her words."

"How?" Cassie asked.

"What *exactly* did she say?" Memorization and attentiveness were areas of special focus with the girl's tutors. It was good seeing what her money paid for.

Cassie furrowed her brow, looking so much like Mort that it made Nancy's throat squeeze shut. "Artemis said, 'My mom read in the paper that your dad was a fugitive. That's a bad guy who's also a coward.' The coward part didn't bother me because I know Daddy isn't one."

Nancy wagged a finger. "But that was your best weapon. An argument is a house of cards. If you can pluck one card from the base, the whole thing falls. You understand?"

The furrow deepened, joined by a crinkling of the nose. "You mean if I told them Daddy killed bad wizards for a living, he couldn't also be a bad guy?"

"You could make the argument that he's not a coward. By invalidating one point of your friend's argument, you'd call into question her other evidence."

"But he isn't, is he?"

"Isn't what?"

"I. Want. Daddy!!!" Cedric shouted. He fell supine, pounding fists and heels on the floor.

With a wave of her hand, Nancy canceled gravity around her son, and he rose, flailing helplessly and ineffectually at nothing. Steadying him just out of reach of the twelve-foot ceiling, she circled a finger and drew a bubble of silence around him as well.

Cassie carried on as if none of it had happened. "A bad guy. Daddy's not a bad guy, right? Because he fought bad guys?"

No lies. They were too young to know the details, but Nancy refused to lie to them on Mort's behalf. Not after what he'd done to her and the kids.

"No, your father is a bad guy."

"Where *were* you boys?" Becky demanded as soon as Chuck stepped aboard the *Radio City* with Brad in tow. She looked past him to the boy. "I thought you were going out for ice cream!"

"I got ice cream," Brad protested.

Chuck tousled the boy's hair. "Go on and get settled. Me and your mom have some grown-up stuff to discuss."

Becky lowered her voice and poked a finger in Chuck's chest. "Not to be a square, but dammit, Chuck. You can't just run off like that."

Keeping his best disarming grin plastered in place, he leaned to peer past her. "The muppets asleep?"

"For like, an hour. I fed 'em three meals while you were gone, old man. I super-mommed the shit out of today. Where in the blessed cosmos *were* you?"

Chuck patted the air with his hands. There was no preventing the beating he was about to take, but he had to try softening the initial blows. "Look. First off, it wasn't my fault."

Fury already brewing, Becky poked him in the chest like a woodpecker looking for grubs. "That has never, ever, *ever* been true! It's always your fault."

"OK. Maybe a little. But I was an innocent bystander. Mistaken identity. Innocent mistake. OK, maybe not so innocent. But the guys who grabbed me thought I was some itinerant freighter captain named Boris—who admittedly bore a striking resemblance based on the picture they showed me. Long story short, Brad intercepted the ransom note they sent and—"

"Brad *WHAT*?"

Anticipating her rushing off to confront their eldest son, Chuck already had a hand ready to catch her by the shoulder and prevent her sudden whirl in the direction of Brad's bunk. "Don't go blaming him. You clearly had super-momming to do."

Becky shut her eyes and repeated a mantra. "Please don't have a police record. Please don't have a police record..."

"Re-laaaaax," he cooed. "Brad's been paying attention. He knew better than to invite the fuzz."

"What am I missing?" Becky asked. She wasn't buying the

sales pitch and Chuck hadn't even finished laying the groundwork. "What did you sign us up for? Are we transporting live organs? Marrying Rhiannon off to a colonial prince? If you try to pull that 'they needed DNA to keep their bloodline alive' bullshit again, I swear I'll—"

"I didn't cut a deal. Brad rescued me."

"Brad..."

Chuck nodded.

"Rescued you..."

"Uh, huh."

"From gangsters?"

"I didn't get their affiliation or anything. But yeah. Some kind of local gang."

"We don't even own a blaster... right?"

Chuck raised his right hand, three fingers up with his thumb pinning his pinkie down. "Scout's honor."

"You're clearly setting up a punchline, and I can't see it. Go ahead. Lay it on me. You're clearly crowing like Peter Pan over this one. Sock it to me."

Somehow, her seeing through the basic idea of the setup sapped some of the joy from springing it on her. But if he let it show, she rained on more of his picnics. Chuck had no choice but to press onward.

"He tracked down Mort."

"The crazy wizard?"

On cue, Mort poked his head in from the passenger stairs. "Hi, Mrs. Ramsey."

Placing a hand over his heart, Chuck made his plea. "He followed me home from a daring rescue that saved my life. Can I keep him?"

Mort received the same scowl that the kids got when

Becky caught them lying. "Did you really save Chuck's life today?"

"In complete honesty, I couldn't say what the kidnappers were planning to do with him. I'm not a mind-reader."

That the wizard delivered the line without a hitch hinted at a gift for lying that began long before this incident. Good. Chuck didn't know what he could do if Mort ever decided to get pissed off at him, so catching him in lies wasn't a major deal. Knowing he could hold his own keeping Becky in the dark over the kind of stuff that relegated him to sleeping on the couch was way more important.

"Also, the method of his liberation involved the—what's a delicate way to put this...?" Mort rubbed his chin between thumb and forefinger a moment before his eyes lit. "Ah. We murdered several people."

Becky's mouth gaped. "Murdered?"

"We?" Chuck added.

"Fine. It was all me. Let's just say there's a mass murder investigation underway, and—"

"*MASS* murder?"

"Eight," Chuck interjected. "Don't go thinking he burned, like, a whole stadium of people alive."

"*BURNED ALIVE*?"

Mort waved a hand to brush the notion aside. "Instantaneous. They felt nothing."

Becky met Chuck's eye, and the conversation continued as a quick series of glares and scowls.

You brought a mass murderer onto this ship? Into our home?

He's a good guy. Only did it to save me.

Find a way to get rid of him.

You tell him.

I'm not the one who brought him here!

I owe him my life.

Chuck's pursed lips and puppy dog eyes carried the day.

Becky wagged a finger. "No killing the tech. The star-drive works now. We'll use it."

Mort held up a hand. "Won't happen again."

"It better not." Becky resigned herself with a huff. "I'm sure Brad's going to be thrilled. I'd offer to tell him, but I'm sure you already did." With that, she headed into their bedroom and shut the door somewhere between a slam and not so loud as to wake the little ones.

Mort nodded. "Just like you said. How soon can we get off this glassteel shopping mall of a planet?"

"Pronto," Chuck replied. "Be in the astral before suppertime."

The wizard wandered into the living room and gave an appraising look. The pitch to Becky had sounded like a quick ride to the next planet, but Chuck had no intention of giving up on a guy who could bail him out of jams and shrink the galaxy to the size of a star system so easily.

Keeping his voice down, Chuck asked, "And since I don't have anyplace I need to head right now... where'd be the best place to find some of that magic obsidian?"

****

Ready for more *Black Ocean: Mirth & Mayhem*?
Grab Mission 2, Low Flyer

BACK MATTER

BOOKS BY J. S. MORIN

Black Ocean

Black Ocean is a vivid 26th century story universe where science and magic coexist—sort of.

Black Ocean: Galaxy Outlaws

Black Ocean: Galaxy Outlaws is a fast-paced fantasy space opera series about the small crew of the *Mobius* trying to squeeze out a living. If you love fantasy and sci-fi, and still lament over the cancellation of *Firefly*, *Black Ocean: Galaxy Outlaws* is the series for you.

Read about the *Black Ocean: Galaxy Outlaws* series and discover where to buy at: galaxyoutlawsmissions.com

Black Ocean: Astral Prime

Co-written with author M.A. Larkin, *Black Ocean: Astral Prime* hearkens back to location-based space sci-fi classics like *Babylon 5* and *Star Trek: Deep Space Nine*. *Astral Prime* builds on the rich *Black Ocean* universe, introducing a colorful cast of characters for new and returning readers alike. Come along for the ride as a minor outpost in the middle of nowhere becomes a key point of interstellar conflict.

Read about the *Black Ocean: Astral Prime* series and discover where to buy at: astralprimemissions.com

Black Ocean: Mercy for Hire

Black Ocean: Mercy for Hire follows the exploits of a pair of do-gooder bounty hunters who care more about saving the day than securing a payday. The series builds on the rich *Black Ocean* universe, centering on a couple of fan-favorites and introducing a colorful cast for new and returning readers alike. Fans of vigilante justice and heroes who exemplify the word will love this series.

Read about *Black Ocean: Mercy for Hire* and discover where to buy at: mercyforhiremissions.com

Black Ocean: Mirth & Mayhem

Black Ocean: Mirth & Mayhem delves into the origins of two vagabonds making their living among the stars. Mort is a wizard coming to grips with a life on the run and estrangement from the comforts and respect he had on Earth. Brad is an impressionable youth, too clever for his—or anyone's—good. And Chuck Ramsey is the mold that Brad's trying to break out of, which is harder than he could ever have dreamed.

Read about *Black Ocean: Mirth & Mayhem* and discover where to buy at: mirthandmayhemmissions.com

Black Ocean: Passage of Time

The year was 2586. A few minutes later, it was 2591. Caught up in a time travel snafu, Eric and Jessie Ramsey become fugitives from the people who want answers as to how they did it—and where their loyalties lie in the galactic war that broke out in their absence.

Read about *Black Ocean: Passage of Time* and discover where to buy at: passageoftimemissions.com

Twinborn Chronicles

The *Twinborn Chronicles* is an epic fantasy saga based on the possibility that our dreams offer us a glimpse into the life of another – another who can get the same glimpse into our world.

Read about the *Twinborn Chronicles* and discover where to buy at: twinbornchronicles.com

Twinborn Chronicles: Awakening

Experience the journey of mundane scribe Kyrus Hinterdale who discovers what it means to be Twinborn—and the dangers of getting caught using magic in a world that thinks it exists only in children's stories.

Twinborn Chronicles: War of 3 Worlds

Then continue on into the world of Korr, where the Mad Tinker and his daughter try to save the humans from the oppressive race of Kuduks. When their war spills over into both Tellurak and Veydrus, what alliances will they need to forge to make sure the right side wins?

Project Transhuman

Project Transhuman brings genetic engineering into a post-apocalyptic Earth, 1000 years aliens obliterated all life.

These days, even the humans are built by robots.

Charlie7 is the oldest robot alive. He's seen everything from the fall of mankind at the hands of alien invaders to the rebuilding of a living world from the algae up. But what he hasn't seen in over a thousand years is a healthy, intelligent human. When Eve stumbles into his life, the old robot finally has something worth coming out of retirement for: someone to protect.

Read about all of the *Project Transhuman* books and discover where to buy at: projecttranshuman.com

Sins of Angels

Co-written with author M.A. Larkin, *Sins of Angels* is an epic space opera series set 3000 years after the fall of Earth. With the scope of *Dune* and the adventurous spirit of *Indiana Jones*, it delivers a conflict that spans galaxies and rests on the spirit of brave researcher Professor Rachel Jordan. Follow the complete saga, and watch as the fate of our species hangs in the balance.

Read about *Sins of Angels* and discover where to buy at: sinsofangelsbooks.com

Shadowblood Heir

Shadowblood Heir explores what would happen if the writer of your favorite epic fantasy TV show died before the show ended—and the show was responsible. If you wonder what it would be like if an epic fantasy world invaded our world, this urban fantasy story might give you that glimpse.

Read about *Shadowblood Heir* and discover where to buy at: shadowbloodheir.com

EMAIL INSIDERS

You made it to the end! Maybe you're just persistent, but hopefully that means you enjoyed the book. But this is just the end of one story. If you'd like reading my books, there are always more on the way!

Perks of being an Email Insider include:

- Notification of book releases (often with discounts)
- Inside track on beta reading
- Advance review copies (ARCs)
- Access to Inside Exclusive bonus extras and giveaways
- Best of my blog about fantasy, science fiction, and the art of worldbuilding

Sign up for the my Email Insiders list at: jsmorin.com/updates

ABOUT THE AUTHOR

I am a creator of worlds and a destroyer of words. As a fantasy writer, my works range from traditional epics to futuristic fantasy with starships. I have worked as an unpaid Little League pitcher, a cashier, a student library aide, a factory grunt, a cubicle drone, and an engineer—there is some overlap in the last two.

Through it all, though, I was always a storyteller. Eventually I started writing books based on the stray stories in my head, and people kept telling me to write more of them. Now, that's all I do for a living.

I enjoy strategy, worldbuilding, and the fantasy author's privilege to make up words. I am a gamer, a joker, and a thinker of sideways thoughts. But I don't dance, can't sing, and my best artistic efforts fall short of your average notebook doodle. When you read my books, you are seeing me at my best.

My ultimate goal is to be both clever and right at the same time. I have it on good authority that I have yet to achieve it.

Connect with me online
jsmorin.com

facebook.com/authorjsmorin

twitter.com/authorjsmorin

bookbub.com/authors/j-s-morin

goodreads.com/JSMorin

tiktok.com/@authorjsmorin

www.ingramcontent.com/pod-product-compliance
Lightning Source LLC
LaVergne TN
LVHW090952080826
845145LV00003B/986

* 9 7 8 1 6 4 3 5 5 1 2 3 4 *